MURDER
AT THE
ART MUSEUM

A NOVEL BY

CHRISTINA SQUIRE

www.abqpress.com

www.abqpress.com

Albuquerque, New Mexico

ISBN 978-1-68418-901-4

Acknowledgements

Many thanks to Lynn C. Miller
and members of my critique group:
Lynda Miller, Laurie Hause, Tina Carlson,
Kim Feldman, and Jill Root.
Their advice, encouragement, and
good humor were invaluable to me.

I wish to thank my publisher Judith Van Gieson
for her patience and support.

I also gratefully acknowledge the
following people for their help:
Michele Penhall, Katherine Johnson-Fickles,
Bruce Squire, Darcey Squire, Pat and Bruce Carpenter,
and Dr. Wilbur Williams.

I have worked at the University Art Museum with some wonderful, talented people. Characters in this book are dramatic creations and pure fiction.

One

"Well? What happened next?" my sister hissed in my ear as we inched passed two people sitting at the end of the first row behind the rail at the movie theatre.

"We walked into the library, Inspector Hutchinson went to one section, and I went to another. That's all." I said over my shoulder as I plopped down in a center seat. I balanced my kiddie pack of popcorn, fruit gummies, and miniscule Diet Coke on my lap. I unwrapped my hot dog and took a huge bite.

"Don't say Inspector Hutchinson in that prissy way, Caro! Spill your guts about James!"

A gob of mustard and relish fell on my blouse. "Shit!" I rubbed the slop off with a napkin. "Nothing happened!" God, my sister was relentless. Didn't she know I'm a long married woman? A mother? What did she think I will do?

I didn't even know what I'll do. And I got dangerously excited thinking about it. But I did not want to admit it to myself or anyone. Yet.

"You didn't talk at all? After all you've been through?" Sally asked.

"A little outside the door."

"A little outside the door," Sally mimicked in a snotty little sister voice. "What did he say?"

"Oh…he was back in New Orleans working on a case. Now he's here investigating another murder on the university campus."

"That hotbed of intrigue! Did he want to see you again?"

"No! Look. Our past was nothing but a classic example of mysterious man awakens a woman sexually. But it was all in my head, honest to you! End of story."

"I don't believe you for a minute!"

"Shush! The movie is starting!"

"Your life has been like a movie, Caro!" Sally whispered.

Yes, my life had been like a grade B movie with characters straight out of Central Casting. But the murder at the observatory was solved, my children were safe, my dog was sweet, and my marriage was stumbling along.

But why did I still think of my inspector every day? Those thoughts unbalanced me. James Hutchinson had led the murder investigation of a prominent astronomy professor. I became a "person of interest" in the case and was thrown into contact with him on a regular basis. Through persistence (and desperation) I helped solve the murder, but not before falling completely under his spell. After a time, I attributed my hot thoughts to a romance novel I was critiquing for a friend at the time and to my long married state. Back to normal at last, whatever that was, I appreciated security, affection, loyalty and a shared history with my husband, but Christ I missed excitement. It was not to be. Not in this life anyway. I had other jewels in my crown.

I lost my crown (and the jewels) when I saw him at Ernie Pyle Library last week. So quickly I turned! I hadn't seen or heard from him for months after the observatory murder. Then there he was picking up the books I dropped. A perfect vision. And my body turned against my contented brain. I burned, I stuttered, my glasses flew off my head, my knees went weak, I stumbled. He picked up my glasses. I put them back on. He offered me his arm. We walked down the sidewalk together. He held all my books as well as his own.

"Let's sit before we go in," James said.

I collapsed on the little bench outside the door like an unstrung puppet. My arm that he held was burning. I just kept looking at his face. My mouth was probably hanging open.

I finally croaked. "How are you?"

"Very well, thank you. How are you?"

" Oh fine. Fine. Fine!"

"How's Max?"

"Oh he's himself! Thank goodness!" My youngest son, Max, suffered a severe blow to the head a few months ago while searching the observatory for the murderer. James found him and rushed him to the emergency room. James also came to our home to visit Max while he was recuperating from the concussion.

"Glad to hear it," he said.

"What have you been up to?"

"I went back to New Orleans for a cold case that I had been working on before I transferred here."

"Did you solve it?"

"No, but I discovered more details. I'll continue the investigation after I finish this one."

"Which one?"

"I'm looking into another murder at the university."

"No kidding! Where? I haven't read about it in the *Albuquerque Journal.*"

"Some murders are never covered, unfortunately. And I can't discuss the case yet."

"So you find out about Albuquerque murders all the way in New Orleans and come here to solve them?"

"The Albuquerque Police Department is short staffed. New Orleans has an exchange program with your city. I applied. Again."

"Why?"

"Because it's the Land of Enchantment." James smiled.

"Is it now," I said.

"Yes, it is."

I had a hot flash. "Well, welcome back and good luck, Inspector Hutchinson." I wanted to throw my arms around him. But I didn't.

"Thank you."

We stood up. James opened the door for me. He put his hand on my waist as I stepped by him. He placed our books on the back room return shelf. Then he abruptly went into the non-fiction room, and I twirled the current fiction books displayed on a Lazy Susan and felt like fainting. I waved at him before I left without checking out any books. I couldn't think. My waist tingled. So much for an assignation. Sparks fly at Ernie Pyle Library. Fizzled more like it.

James Hutchinson still drove me crazy no matter how much I loved what I had. No matter how much I re-read *A Grateful Heart*. When I got home I logged on to the University job line. For some reason.

***

My first interview was with the University Art Museum. Such refined people. Such closed lipped smiles. Such soft, cultured voices. Such plummy vowel sounds. Such severe bob hairdos. Such stylish, tailored clothes. I was hired even though I wore Griffin earrings.

I landed a dream job: Museum Shop Manager. And only part-time! Perfect in every way! Sitting at the entrance, surrounded by art, greeting sensitive art lovers, answering intelligent questions over the phone, and buying exciting, tasteful merchandise to sell, and hosting grand openings. And I got to look arty! What's not to like? I could leave in the afternoon in time to greet my charming sons home from school, walk my dog, rustle up dinner for everyone, and read my library books. Balance in one's day is the key! I thought I had life all figured out.

Two

"You're going to go back THERE?" my husband asked.

"Yes. And it's a dream job! What's wrong with an art museum?" I said.

"After how the University of New Mexico treated you? Are you a glutton for punishment?"

"Excuse me. The Art Museum is not a department. It's filled with cultured people who appreciate quality. Academic egos play no part here! And they chose me. I am happy. Why can't you be?"

John and I were on our back deck having our wine and few ciggies before dinner. I stared at his tall, distinguished figure stretched out between two lawn chairs. In all his pontificating glory.

"I think you're making a big mistake. Stay away from that place! The people in power want to look good no matter what the cost. It's a bureaucratic spider's web. You should know that by now."

"Well, not everyone can work in their Daddy's accounting practice where everyone loves each other," I said.

"Touche," he said and clinked my wine glass. "I wish you well…but when will you be home everyday?"

"In time to fry up the bacon in a pan, Butt."

***

I ladled green chili stew into bowls as John, Max, and Douglas sat around the kitchen table. I took the warm flour tortillas out of the oven, put out butter, grated cheddar cheese, ripe olives, and sour cream, poured iced tea and milk. I sat down and looked at Douglas, my middle son who was a high school senior, musician, and all-state drummer. He was beating out a silent rhythm on his thigh with his left hand. Max was shoveling stew in his mouth with a dreamy expression in his eyes. Was he stoned? I'll never know. My eldest son, Peter, was eating God knows what at the dorm cafeteria at the University of Texas at Austin.

"Your mother got a job at the University Art Museum," I said to whoever was listening.

"That hotbed of intrigue?" Max asked.

"That's what Aunt Sally said," I replied.

"Congratulations, Mom!" Douglas said. "What will you being doing?"

"Sitting at the front of the museum, greeting visitors, answering the phone, promoting our exhibitions to the public…."

"Ah, Art," Max whispered as he held up a piece of potato on a knife. He raised his other hand in tribute.

"Just eat your food," my husband snapped. Max saluted his Dad as he swallowed the potato.

Max said, "What time will you be home, Mom?"

"When school is out."

"Brilliant!" Max said.

***

I stressed over what to wear on my first day of work. Everyone there is so chic! I decided on black slacks, a white blouse, and black sweater vest. I had to wear my stupid black patent leather Dansko clogs. Note to go shopping! My hair was too short for a chic bob! I'll flatten it out like a cap with Bed Head Manipulator. I will look seriously edgy. Lots of black eyeliner. Crushed berry lips. Chanel Vendetta nail polish. I'm good to go.

Three

Since I had no UNM parking sticker I parked my VW Beetle on a side street next to the Walgreen's on Central and Girard promptly at 8:45 AM. I jumped out of my car, breathed in the exhaust fumes, and thought about all the weight I will lose walking six blocks to and from work everyday. Every step counts! I was so happy to walk through the doors of the Fine Arts Center, across the spacious foyer and up to the Art Museum doors.

Which were locked. What the...? Oh, of course! The Art Museum was closed on Mondays! I have to learn to read signs. But I was told to report today at 9 AM. I walked down a long hall, up the steps and tried to open the door to the administrative office. It was locked. What the...? I knocked timidly. Did not want to disturb artistic sensibilities. No response. I knocked louder. Nothing. I pounded. The door opened. There stood an obese woman holding a huge to go Styrofoam mug.

"Can I help you?" she asked and took a slurp.

"Hi! I'm Caroline Steele! I'm the new Museum Shop--"

"Yeah. I heard we finally hired someone."

I put my happy face on. "I'm supposed to meet Pat in the Art Museum. It's locked."

"I'm on the phone."

She looked me up and down. I looked her up and down. She was wearing gray sweatpants, a red Lobo sweatshirt, and white tennis shoes.

She turned around and walked away from me. Agh! Rude! Hoping to find a cultured, friendly staff member, I followed her massive figure. I passed four closed doors with the plaques: DIRECTOR, ASSISTANT DIRECTOR, REGISTRAR, PUBLICITY. My interview was held in a Fine Arts College conference room, so I was lost here. I heard her talking on the phone. I followed the voice to a high walled, black cubicle.

"Listen. Gotta go," she said. "The new gal is here. Yeah...I know...heh heh."

She came around the barricade holding a huge key ring. "I'm Linda." She squeezed past me. "I'll let you into the museum. You need to fill out key cards, bring them to the Physical Plant, and get your own set. I can't be doing this for you all the time."

"OK, Linda," I said to her broad back. "Where is everybody?"

"Meeting with the police."

"What happened?"

"Some homeless guy was found dead in our handicapped lift."

"Oh my God!"

"Ach! They roam all over this building. Probably died of alcohol poisoning."

"Are the city police involved?" I asked in a high voice as I followed her down a hall. She was surprisingly fast on her feet.

"They better be. The campus police are like Keystone Cops."

"Haha!" I said.

No reply.

Linda unlocked the door to the museum. Air whooshed in. It was like the gallery was vacuum packed. Only a few dim overhead lights were on. The front desk and shop were dark. The air was cold. I felt like I was walking into a crypt.

Four

"Well, I guess I'm your welcoming committee," Linda said. "Pat is probably talking to the police. I'll show you around."

I was totally taken aback dressed up in all my edginess. My first day certainly did not seem to be a priority among the ruling class. But murder was murder. I should know that by now.

"So this is the front desk where you'll sit. Around the corner you can see the book room. There's a storage closet in back. Pat can show you all the shop stuff."

I walked by the desk with little baskets full of ugly ceramic jewelry for sale. One was filled with Mona Lisa refrigerator magnets. No imagination, I thought.

We walked down seven steps into the main gallery. Huge, high-walled ceilings. Ugly tile floors. But exciting photography on the walls. I started to look around.

"You'll have plenty of time to stare at that stuff," Linda said. Her voice echoed in the huge, dark expanse.

"Let's go downstairs to the lower galleries. We turned right and started walking down a spiral staircase. Huge works of a crucified, bleeding Jesus and speared, bleeding saints hung on the side wall. "We are famous for our Spanish Colonial Art," she said and waved her hand at the paintings without looking at them. The lower space had architect drawings from 19th century Paris. A large closet sized gallery to the left had 19th century photographs of dead children in elaborate little coffins. What an upper.

I was feeling claustrophobic. This airless space smelled musty: like dirty, wet carpet or wet, dirty dog. The walls seemed to close in on me. I felt like I was in a cavern.

Linda pointed to a door in the corner. "That's the Print Study Room where our photography collection is kept. The Curator of Photography has an office in there." A big roach crawled in front of us. Linda stomped on it. "Watch out. They fly." We started to go back up the stairs when I heard voices coming from another door opposite from where we were standing.

"What does that lead to?" I asked.

"Oh. That's the handicapped lift. That's where the stiff was found. You are going to have to wheel people from the upper gallery down here. Part of your job, you know."

"Oh. Yes." In fact, I did not know. Who is going to mind the museum while I did that? I was forming some questions in my poor mind. And rethinking my wardrobe and shoe choice.

Linda pointed to a large double door. "There is where they bring in exhibitions for our lower galleries."

We ascended the spiral staircase. I was so relieved to leave this grim underbelly. Linda was huffing and puffing. She walked to the far end of the main gallery. We turned right and walked up a few more steps in a long, narrow exhibition space with another photography show of the Depression Era skeletal families sitting on rickety porches dressed in rags.

"These were commissioned by the WPA," Linda said. "We take pride in these original prints."

"It's amazing what people went through then," I whispered. "So sad."

"Yeah, well, shows the times, doesn't it?"

"Yeah, well, you wouldn't want anything uplifting."

Linda stared at me. I stared back.

I turned to a glass door to the foyer at one end. "For handicapped access," Linda said.

We returned to the main gallery. She opened a tall, wide double door at the back. We were at the exit to a loading dock on one side and an elevator on the other. She pointed to a closed door in the middle. "Shipping and receiving," she gasped. "Our collection is stored under it. You'll never go down there." We took the elevator down to the basement. Another closed, unmarked door was immediately to our left. "The Art Museum bathroom. You'll need a key." Everything in this place was locked up, I thought. Closed. Protected from the public. Sealed like a tomb. A maze. I blinked my eyes in the low neon overhead lighting. Everything looked ghostly. Our footsteps bounced off the discolored walls. The hair stood up on the back of my neck. Was this the Hotel California? I could check out any time I liked, but I could never leave?

We walked down a long hall to another closed locked door. She opened it with a key. Zydeco music blasted. It was the size of an airplane hangar: long tables with hammers, nails, empty frames, levelers, planks of wood, and various sharp cutting devices hung from floor to ceiling. "The Curator of Exhibitions works here. He hangs and frames all of our shows. KEN!" Linda screamed. I jumped. "He must be with the rest of them. Let's go to the hall entrance to the lower gallery. I'll show you the door to the handicapped lift."

She stopped and turned to me. "You are responsible for the security of all the art galleries."

"Huh?"

"Pat will show you the TV screens behind the desk. Didn't you notice all the cameras in our four galleries?"

"Oh. Those." I lied.

"Well. You have to pay attention! We don't alarm our art here!"

My head was spinning. My ears were ringing. My edginess was ground down to a nub. I hung my head and matched Linda's heavy tread. What have I gotten into? Again. We turned a corner. So did Inspector James Hutchinson.

Five

I plowed right into him. I went down. James grabbed my arms. I grabbed his arms. He pulled me up.

"Mrs. Steele. What a surprise."

I could not speak.

"So you two know each other?" Linda asked.

"Kinda sorta," I whispered as I gazed into his eyes.

We kept a hold on each other. I finally tore myself away from his green eyes. I looked over his shoulder and saw six people staring at me.

I turned away from James and addressed the group standing behind us.

"Hello!" I said. "Linda was giving me a tour!"

Silence.

A tall, thin man with gray hair and Van Dyke beard stepped forward with his hand outstretched. He wore shorts and a tee shirt. There were sweat stains under his arms. "Hi. I'm Roland Walters, Museum Director.

You must be Caroline."

"I am." I shook his hand.

"Glad Linda could greet you. We are involved in some nasty business. She probably told you all about it. I will put you in to the capable hands of Pat, your job share partner."

Everyone but Pat and James filed past me. Without a glance. And three of the women along with Pat had interviewed me! I felt like chopped liver.

Pat had on jeans, a plaid shirt, and tennis shoes. Well, it was a Monday. I felt so overdressed, overdone, and overwrought. I was finished for the day, and it wasn't even noon. I looked at my inspector dressed as usual like a Banana Republic model.

"Good to see you, as always, Mrs. Steele," he said. "Congratulations on your new job." He walked down the hall. I had this overwhelming urge to run after him, jump into his arms, and never see my family or UNM again. I took a deep breath.

"He is so nice!" Pat said watching James go. "So you know him?"

"I met him when he was investigating a murder at Physics and Astronomy. I used to work there."

"Lucky you. For knowing him, I mean. Not working at Physics and Astronomy!"

"They both have their charms."

"Well, I hope he solves this horrible situation." She put her arm around my waist. "Let's go upstairs and talk. Linda probably scared you!"

"She's rather intense."

"She's a pussycat, really. Linda has to hold her own around all these egos."

I thought the university was filled with inflated egos. "What about this dead man? Who was he? Was he murdered?"

"Yes. His name was Charles Lowry. He was homeless and used to visit the Art Museum. He was quite mad. But he didn't deserve to be bludgeoned to death and dumped in a lift."

"Charles Lowry? That name is familiar. Didn't he teach in the Art and Art History Department? I had a Contemporary Art class taught by a Charles Lowry years ago," I said.

"Oh yes…when he was first hired he had to teach introduction to art classes, art appreciation…the powers that be load up the newbies…make them pay their dues. But until he had to leave, Charles taught the advanced painting classes. He was also commercially successful. Not many art teachers are. I'm sorry to say."

"I remember he invited the whole class up to his land in El Morro at the end of the semester, " I said. "He just had an Airstream trailer at the time, but he put up a big tent, roasted a pig, and had a band. Charles was so full of life. And so creative and generous."

"He was very popular…for while there," Pat said as we walked down the hall.

"Every time I walk into a museum I think about Professor Lowry's class. I appreciate art so much because of him."

"I guess he affected many lives…" Pat nodded.

"How did he end up homeless? I can't believe it!"

"It's a sad story, Caroline. But we have a lot to do this morning. We'll talk about Charles later, OK?"

"How did he get in the handicapped lift?" I pressed on as we walked quickly down the hall.

"Someone must have left that access door unlocked. It's awful."

"How many people have keys to that door?"

"Oh Caroline! You detective, you! I'm sure Inspector Hutchinson is looking into that."

"He's very thorough," I murmured.

We took the elevator up to the main gallery. Pat brought another chair for me to sit with her behind the front desk.

"Here is the phone. Duh! You have to answer all the calls coming to the museum. You forward the calls for the administrative staff to each of them. There's the phone list. Here are the video screens. You have to watch for bad behavior!"

"What do I do?"

"Tell them to stop," she answered.

"What if it's downstairs or in the side gallery?"

"Walk over there and tell them to stop."

"But I'll have to leave the front desk."

"You'll have a student employee with you at all times."

"I will?"

"That reminds me. We have to post student job openings. I'll do that this afternoon. My helpers have left. We must interview!"

I had never interviewed anyone in my life.

"You have to do a security check on each applicant. The campus police do it. The Art Museum needs students! They must staff it Tuesday nights and Sunday afternoons. You certainly don't want to!" She opened a drawer. "Here is the cash box. You must count the money you made during the week every Monday and deposit it at the cashier's office. Here is the credit card machine. You must add up all the slips every week. Here is the counter. You must count every visitor and hand the total in to the office every Monday." She pointed to a large plastic box by the front door. "There is the donation box. You must count all the money every Monday and turn it in to the office."

My God! Another responsibility. What do those people behind that locked door do? At least the museum is closed Mondays, I rationalized. I was not chained to the front desk. But I had to still be the switchboard operator for seven people. Oh yes, I rationalized once again. I'd have a student worker by then.

Pat got up. "Let me show you the storage closet." We passed through the book room full of dusty art journals and exhibition catalogues. She opened a door in the back. The space had empty metal shelves, an old office chair, and a pile of boxes. "If you like to shop, you can order more stuff to sell out front. I can't be bothered. You have to get a purchasing clearance."

"Oh I love to shop!"

"Here is the fuse box. You switch on the gallery lights here."

I watched as she pointed at the many switches.

"I keep my purse in here," she said, closed the door, and locked it.

20

"You need to get keys for the front door of the art museum, our bathroom, the administration office, the storage closet, and the downstairs handicapped lift."

"Linda told me."

"Do it this afternoon."

"Ok."

"Remember Caroline: Often the one at the front desk of the Art Museum is the first person a visitor sees at the university. We may be the face of the university! We must attend! We must be friendly. Some people love to talk, you know."

"Oh I know." I can certainly talk with the best of them. And answer phones, and police this sprawling dungeon, sell stuff, order stuff, count money, manage student help, and be perky. I was so glad this was a part-time job. I didn't know how Pat used to do this all day.

"So when you come in tomorrow turn on the lights and open the front doors. Ready for business!"

"What if I have to go to the bathroom, and I'm alone?"

"Just call Linda. She'll sit down here."

Six

I left Pat and walked to the administrative office. Locked. I knocked with energy. The door opened.

"What?" Linda demanded.

"I'm here to get key cards. Please."

"It's lunch time."

"I am supposed to work until 1. It's 12:30. I have to have keys before I come tomorrow. Which means I have to walk across campus to the Physical Plant. Or you can let me into the museum again, of course."

She turned abruptly around. I followed Linda to her fortress. She plopped down in her chair, yanked open a drawer, pulled out green key cards, shoved a MacDonald's bag over with her elbow to make room on her desk, and started filling in spaces.

"I need five keys to--"

"I know what you need," she said.

Oh no you don't, I thought.

She handed me the cards. "You have to have the director sign this. He's out playing tennis. So wait." She dug in her bag and took out a french fry. I was so hungry and tired. I wanted to cry. Why did I do the things I do?

"Where should I wait?" I asked.

"Wherever."

"Thank you."

Since there were no seats anywhere to be seen, and I looked at four sealed doors all around me, I went out to the foyer and sat on a bench so I could watch anyone going into the art museum office. I was making a big mistake. I took out a little spiral notebook in my purse with a 1950s Spam ad on the cover. I started writing down my thoughts: I better get out of this while I can. I do not need to be in this situation. I don't need the money, thank you husband! I don't need the stress. Back at UNM all because I wanted the possibility of seeing James again. Or was I bored? Making rash decisions? Why can't I make fun rash decisions? Like oh flying off to Paris? Oh no! I have to accept jobs that torture me. At the mercy of weird people. I need therapy. What was the chance James was investigating a murder where I just got a job? Is this a sign? Or a karmic backlash? I am so tired of myself. I am going to tell the director I am not taking this job--

"Be careful what you write." My Inspector sat down next to me. "I may have to confiscate another notebook."

"What I'm writing will not incriminate me this time," I said and turned beet red remembering the murder investigation at my former job.

"But I bet it will delight me," he said.

"I have no doubt."

"Want a peach?" James pulled one out of his jacket pocket.

"Where did you get that?"

"La Montanita Coop has a satellite location in the Bookstore. It's organic. And happy."

"Well, that's a relief," I took the peach. "Thank you." I had a big bite. "I am so hungry," I said with my mouth full. Juice ran down my chin. I wiped the back of my hand over my lips and handed the dripping peach back to him.

James looked at me. He took a bite.

"Well! If it isn't my new museum shop lady!" Roland boomed as he walked up to us swinging a tennis racket.

I swallowed the sweet fruit. "Will you please sign my key cards?"

Seven

"Better go to the Physical Plant," I said as I stood up. My Inspector stood up also. I ratcheted around in my purse for my pearl white Vogue cat eye sunglasses. He reached in his pocket for his black Ray Bans and covered up those beautiful green eyes.

"Shall we?" he said and offered his arm. I slipped my hand through it. His jacket was soft and nubby.

"We shall," I replied. I was surprised that James wanted to go with me. But who was I to question this moment?

We walked out of the Fine Arts Center past the Student Union Building. What a beautiful day. Loud tinny music came from a homeless man in the middle of the mall holding a boom box high up in the air. He started singing off key and dancing like a whirling dervish.

"Never a dull moment around here," I said, stupidly, breaking the silence.

"Never a dull moment in Albuquerque, period," James said.

We turned left and went down the steps to another expanse of concrete: Zimmerman Library on our right, the Humanities Building on our left, and Mitchell Hall straight ahead. As we passed the library the green, gently rolling hills around the Duck Pond came into view. I was so tired but exhilarated. I felt light-headed but full-bodied. I was hot. I didn't know what I was. I couldn't talk. I didn't know what I was doing. Oh yes. Getting keys to work in a mausoleum. And holding on to James.

We walked by a hot dog vendor.

"Want a hot dog?" James asked.

"I love hot dogs!"

We brought our wrapped hot dogs, bags of chips and cokes to the Duck Pond. James took off his jacket and placed it on the plush grass near the water. I kicked off my clogs. I wanted to kick everything off my body. But instead I sat down on the soft tweed fabric. I started to take demure bites and worried about getting bun stuck in my teeth. James pulled off some bread and threw it to the few ducks that swam up to us quacking loudly. All around us students read, talked head to head, slept, or sunbathed.

We ate our lunch in silence. James threw our trash away. He sat back down next to me. A man of few words, I thought, as I looked at him. But I knew better. Perhaps our conversations last year only revolved around the murder at the observatory. And we now were at a loss. But only for words, apparently, because as he lay back on the grass, he took my hands and pulled me to him. I eased down beside him on my stomach and propped myself up on my elbows close to his face. I took off his shades. He took off mine. I raised a hand to wipe a bit of mustard off his chin and showed him. James put my finger in his mouth. And bit.

"Mom! Hello!" I spun around nearly spraining my back to see Max standing over us. I shot up. James slowly rose to his feet.

"What are you doing here?" I demanded. "Why aren't you in school?"

"Mom! I told you that my biology class was going on a field trip to the University Arboratum!"

James and Max shook hands. "How are you, Max?" James said.

"Fine!" Max said. He turned to me. "What are you doing here?"

"I had lunch with Inspector Hutchinson. We're discussing a case."

"Another murder? Radical!"

"At the art museum…"

"And you had to whisper, or what were you doing--?"

"Never mind, Butt. Where's the rest of your class?"

Max pointed across the pond to kids rolling down hills and chasing frightened ducks into the water.

"I've got to get some keys. See you at home, Max. Nice to see you again, Inspector," I said. I walked away. I sucked on my bitten finger. I turned around and went back. James and Max were laughing about something, but they stopped to watch while I found my clogs.

Eight

Well, I've had my exercise today, I thought as I collapsed on the couch. I walked all the way to the Physical Plant that was halfway up the hill to the Campus Observatory and then back to my car. I knew the man who dispensed keys since I had to check out and return keys when I worked at Physics and Astronomy.

"What are you? A glutton for punishment?" he asked as I presented my key cards.

I laughed.

"No really," he continued. "Are you divorced?"

"No."

"Then why are you back working in this place?"

"Something to do," I said.

He shook his head as he handed over the keys to the torture chamber.

***

Now at home I stretched out blissfully braless in my yoga pants and tee shirt and thought about my Inspector. His bite sent an electric charge running through my body. He wanted me. And I wanted him. What will I do? I had children, a dog, a house, and a husband. Will I risk losing them all for ten minutes of bliss? OK hours. Days. Months. Years. A new life with someone who is practically a stranger? I could not go there now. I did not have to. I will practice mindfulness. Here is now.

The boys will be home soon. Then John. Then dinner. No time to daydream. But I'll visualize while I can. I'll have a moment. I swooned. My arm hung off the couch. My fingers brushed the corner of a book. Sight unseen, I lifted the top cover and ruffled hundreds of pages. I rolled over to look down. Oh no. Another manuscript from Tina. Hidden under the couch. I forgot it was there. She brought it to me last week and will be waiting for a response. "This one's different!" she said. "Read it and weep." Tina is a writer and good friend. Last year I plowed through her western bodice ripper novel called *The Love Crescent*. She was still trying to get it published. No one had answered her many query letters. It was sad. But, undaunted, Tina wrote another book. I admired her persistence even as I shoved her heavy tome back under the sofa. I closed my eyes. I went somewhere else.

I woke up. "Hard day at the Art Museum?" John asked.

"Hard day at the Duck Pond?" Max asked.

"What's for dinner, Mom?" Douglas asked.

John, Max and Douglas were in a line looming over my limp body.

"Fish sticks and tater tots!" I said and sat up.

"Oh Mom!" the boys moaned in unison.

"Hey! I'll make my wonderful homemade tarter sauce with catsup and mayo!" I said.

"I forgot that I have band practice tonight. I'll stop by Taco Smell," said Douglas.

"I forgot that I volunteered to pull weeds in the church garden. They're bringing in pizza!" Max shot out the door.

"Ah. That's one way to empty a room," my husband said. "More fish sticks for us!"

I rolled my eyes.

"Just kidding! Let's go out. You can tell me all about the art world. And what you were doing at the Duck Pond."

Nine

I climbed into bed after a hot bath. I could not sleep. I was thinking about how my finger felt in James' mouth. I wanted more. Douglas and Max were in their rooms. John was in his orthopedic Finnish chair in the den watching TV. I did not have the energy to write in my fear journal. I could start reading Tina's manuscript, so I walked to the den. John was snoring in front of a baseball game. Too much wine at Scalo. We talked about the weird Art Museum people and the murdered homeless man. The very same Inspector Hutchinson was investigating. Amazing, huh? How he walked me halfway to pick up my keys. We had a hot dog at the Duck Pond and reminisced about the Campus Observatory case. John talked about his difficulties with a business partner. I was an active-listener, as usual.

I knelt down and dragged out the manuscript. I blew dust and dog hair off the front. Here goes nothing. I stacked more pillows behind me in bed. I had to sit up to hold this massive work. I started.

A Cinnamon Summer

She pressed hard on the gas pedal. Her little Camry hiccupped and surged ahead of the giant semi truck on the Long Island Expressway. Lily blinked her eyes. Was it raining? She could hardly see out the window. She turned on her windshield wipers. They screeched over dry glass. But no. She was crying again. Lily dabbed her violet eyes with the violet floral embroidered hankie she always kept in her bra. Like her grandmother did. Oh if only she could put her head in Grandma Edna's lap! Oh if she could hear her soft voice saying everything will be all right, beautiful child.

But Lily was an adult now. Hoping to begin anew. Hoping to put her past behind her. Hoping to finally get free of a barren, toxic marriage. Hoping to heal from the devastating loss of both parents. Just hoping for she knew not what. But anything would be better than what she had been through. She blew her nose and shook her golden curls. "What am I doing?" She shouted and pounded the steering wheel. Then she took a huge Pilates breath into her back ribs. "Put on your big girl pants!" she shouted to herself. Her words flew out the open windows into the universe. "Is anyone listening?" Lily whispered.

(Oh life is hard, little weepy thing! No children to care for, you have a car, you've suffered loss? Join the club.)

She felt a wet velvet tongue lick her right arm. "Thank you, Tulip! I love you, too!" She reached over to pet her boxer. "We can do this!" Lily said. Tulip sat up straighter in the passenger seat. "You look so dignified," Lily told her precious dog. She laughed through her tears. Her dimples winked at last.

How could this happen to her, she asked herself for the millionth time. As the scenery sped by she went over and over what went wrong with her and Brad. How could he leave her for his secretary? She and Brad were high school sweethearts: He, an athlete scholar and homecoming king and she, Honor Society president and Queen of May. Lily wore Brad's letter jacket proudly through the halls of high school even though it fell below her knees and made her sweat under her armpits.

(Like John and me…but he was no athlete. And I was no Queen of May.)

After graduation they attended different colleges, but Lily hopped on a greyhound bus every break to visit Brad in Colorado. She held on to her virginity as long as she could!

(Oh didn't we all.)

And Brad said that he was suffering so!

(Oh didn't they all.)

This made her sad. So they made sloppy, awkward love every chance they got. Lily was rather underwhelmed but thought this was the way things were supposed to be. What did she know? And she loved Brad.

(I knew nothing. Haven't learned much.)

But her college grades fell. She learned to drink and smoke.

(Who didn't?)

She was nervous so far away from him. Other men asked her out and she went, but no one was like Brad.

(Maybe she had a virgin obsessed mother, so she was damaged goods for anyone else.)

They married shortly after graduating. They bought a little house in the Dallas historical district near the old-fashioned trolley tracks. Lily loved the front yard surrounded by a white picket fence. She planted yellow roses, blue bonnets and daffodils. She started a compost pile in the back yard for her summer garden of tomatoes, peppers, and beans. She ripped out the old shag carpet with her bare hands and found beautiful hardwood floors underneath. Lily had them re-finished and accented the house throughout with bright, ethnic area rugs. She sewed white linen curtains for the shuttered windows.

Brad joined his father's real estate business. Lily spent time every day with her widowed, ailing father who lived alone in the house where she was raised. She shopped for his groceries, cooked dinners for him, drove him to doctor's appointments, and sat with him in total comfort and love.

Her father's recent death devastated her. She was not ready to lose him. Are we ever ready to lose a parent? No, she thought, and started to think on the good memories to dry her tears: Trimming his beard, laughing together at Frasier re-runs, watching him devour her pecan pie, and his face lighting up with mischief as he snatched a cookie off a baking sheet just out of the oven. His illness and dementia did not interfere with his appetite! She baked pies, cakes, and cookies for him and her neighbors. Baking soothed her.

(I only baked chocolate chip cookies at Christmas.)

"Sugar is poison," Brad said. And "You're getting fat!" The delectable smells of her creations took her mind off a less than fulfilling life with Brad who was always working, lifting weights at the gym, running marathons, or going to board meetings.

He jogged while dragging a car tire attached to a chain around his waist. Their sex life became a grim exercise. "Why aren't you pregnant yet?" He'd demand as he spilled his seed into her unceremoniously. "I don't know!" she'd gasp as his long, muscle sculpted body collapsed onto hers. Lily had taken all the fertility tests. She was fine. Brad refused to get checked out. "Men in my family are all fertile!" he'd sneer. "It's got to be you."

(Never had any trouble there! Peter, Douglas, and Max came along as planned.)

Thinking of baked goods made Lily hungry. She did not see any fast food restaurants once she got past New York City. How refreshing! She was on her way to Greenport, Long Island, a small town near the tip of the North Fork, to live with her Aunt Geneva. Her Father's sister enthusiastically invited her to stay as long as she wanted. Geneva did not press for details, to Lily's relief. Lily called her as a last resort. She had no place else to go. She had to get away from her husband Brad. Lily looked forward to spending time with her maiden aunt whom she hadn't seen since she was twelve. She imagined spending quiet, peaceful days with the octogenarian.

Near the ocean. Soaking up the healing negative ions. With no men around.

(I wished I had an Aunt Geneva to stay with when times got rough with John over the years. I had no relatives left except my sister in town. When I was distraught, I drove to the Nature Center, sat on the banks of the Rio Grande River, and stared at the water for over an hour. Calmed me down.)

The Expressway turned into the state road to Greenport. Entering the town of Jamesport she pulled into the parking lot of Grana Italian Restaurant. Lily put her forehead on top of the steering wheel and sighed. She looked down at her petite foot on the brake pedal. She was wearing pink Havaiana flip-flops. Her toenails were painted Chanel Blue Boy with a tiny dolphin decal on each of her big toes. She was glad she got a pedicure before she left Dallas. But who will care? Tulip licked her cheek.

Well, enough of that, I thought as I heaved the book onto my bedside table. I turned off the light. Dolphin decals. Give me a break.

Ten

I arrived at the Art Museum at 8:30 in the morning. Pat was there, thank goodness. She followed me as I prepared for opening at nine. I turned on the lights in the main and lower galleries. We walked around checking the floor for debris. We were janitors, too, apparently. I uncovered the donation box. I straightened the pamphlets in the bookshelves. I felt all good.

"Open the doors, Caro!" Pat said.

There were a few people sitting on benches in the foyer waiting to get in. I boomed "Welcome to the Art Museum" as they filed by. I counted each one on my clicker. That wasn't hard. Pat was sitting to the side of the front desk. She gestured for me to sit behind it. I felt so official. I looked at the security TVs. The visitors were milling around and behaving themselves. How civilized. I can do this, I thought. The phone rang. I answered it in my most pleasing voice. He wanted to talk to the director. I deftly forwarded the call to Roland.

The phone rang again. "I was cut off! I need to speak to Roland!"

"I'm so sorry!" I answered. I transferred again.

"Do you have any books on Fauvism?" a woman demanded in front of the desk.

"Fauvism? I don't know." I drew a blank.

The phone rang. The caller yelled "What's your name? You cut me off again! Do you know who I am…?" I started sputtering apologies.

"You don't know what Fauvism is? And you work in an art museum? Really!" She stomped out the front door.

"Tell me your name! I'm reporting you! You are wasting my time and…" he ranted in my ear.

Pat took the phone from me. "Hi, this is Pat. Can I help you? I know Dr. Jennings. I know. We have a new person here. Caro is learning…yes. Caroline Steele. Yes. Right away." Pat punched a few numbers in.

"What a maniac!" I said.

"And a major donor," she said. "Let me show you how to use this phone."

"This is a different system than what we had at Physics and Astronomy," I said when she was done.

"Sorry. I should have gone over this with you."

"How are you, my little missies?" I looked up to see a decrepit, dirty man shuffling into the museum. He reeked of body odor and alcohol. "Have anything for poor Leroy today?" he lisped. He leaned over the desk and gave me a toothless, black-gummed smile.

I was speechless. Pat went around to the book room closet where we kept our purses. She came back with a dollar bill.

"Get some coffee at McDonald's," she said.

"Ah, that's not enough...come on!" Leroy whined. But he left.

I watched him go. His body odor lingered in the air.

"Did Leroy know the murdered man?" I asked Pat.

"Oh yes. He and Charles became great pals while teaching in the Art Department."

"What happened? Did they retire? Why were they homeless? What about the UNM retirement fund..."

"Hold on, Caro," Pat interrupted. "You are assuming that these men were normal faculty members."

"Actually, I've never known a normal faculty member, Pat."

"Oh Caro! You are so funny! Remember to keep that sunny sense of humor here!"

"I'll try my best, Pat...so just how abnormal were these men?"

Pat looked around the desk, at the lower gallery, the video cameras, and the front door. Visitors were either downstairs or at the far side of the gallery. She rolled her chair close to mine.

"Well," Pat whispered, "Leroy had, has, a drinking problem. He'd show up for classes drunk. The chair gave him many warnings. He threw tantrums in the department offices. The students wanted him fired. They protested in front of the Fine Arts Center. This was very bad publicity! And Leroy was such a wonderful artist in his own right. But he went before a committee and was fired even though he had tenure. Very messy. He took out his retirement. but I don't know what he did with it. Probably paid his wife off after she left him."

"What about Charles?" I asked.

"Oh! Two women accused him of sexual harassment," Pat said. "I always liked him." She looked over my shoulder and smiled. I turned around quickly. Roland was walking in. I smiled, too.

"How's our new little recruit doing?" he boomed.

I bounced up. "Wonderful! What a great museum! And Pat is so patient and helpful!"

"Fabu!" Roland sprinted down the steps and out the back gallery door.

"Now what about Charles?" I sat down. Pat watched as the Director closed the door.

"He also had tenure. And was a renowned artist. He denied the charges but to no avail. The committee fired him. He built a cabin near Grants and lived like a hermit. People say he had a nervous breakdown when his cabin and studio burned down. He came back to Albuquerque last year and wandered around this building spending hours in the Fine Arts Library, lurking around the Art Department, and came in here, of course. Often the campus police were called. I always liked him…"

"Do you think the charges were true?"

"I don't know. The girls who accused him left before graduating. But those in power believed them."

"Administrators! What do they know about what goes on in departments!" I said.

"Not all of them believed the evidence, Caro. Roland cast the deciding vote."

"Why was he on the committee?"

"The Art Museum is not an academic department. We answer to the provost. The Art Museum Director is part of the university administration."

Eleven

"Do you always give Leroy money?" I asked when Pat pointed to the Lower Gallery TV screen. A man was touching a piece of art.

"Get down there," she told me.

I jumped up and ran down the stairs. "Step away from the art!" I said in my stern mother voice.

"OK! Don't get your knickers in a twist," he said.

I returned to the front desk out of breath when Linda marched in. She did not look happy.

"You upset Dr. Jennings."

"He was rude to me."

"He is our biggest donor, and you should have been nicer to him."

"I didn't know who he was!"

"Well, now you do!"

Pat broke in. "She was not familiar with our phone system. We've gone over it now."

Linda looked me up and down and lumbered through the door just as a group of elderly women entered.

"Are you clicking people in?" Pat asked. I grabbed the device.

"Oh look at the magnets!" one woman said as she pawed through the basket. "I'll take this one." She handed me a Mona Lisa with a $50.00 bill.

"Do you have anything smaller?" I asked.

The phone rang. "Excuse me, please," I said as the senior citizen glared at me.

"Curator of Photography? One moment" I trilled and expertly forwarded the call.

"Forget it," the lady said and left the magnet on the desk.

Another woman wanted to buy a book on Andy Warhol. "You know I was married to Andy," she leaned over the counter and whispered.

"Oh really?" I whispered back in an awestruck voice. My acting background always came in handy. All the world is a stage, after all.

"And let me tell you! He was not gay! He loved these!" She lifted up her very large breasts and jiggled them up and down.

"I bet he did," I said. My ears were ringing. She winked at me.

There went the phone. Someone wanted to know about our exhibitions. I put the receiver down to search for a brochure. I did not know the names of all the shows yet. Pat handed me one. I started reading to the caller.

"I want to buy my honey's book!" Andy's widow shouted.

Pat sold her the book while I left to go to the restroom. I splashed water on my face. What a crazy place! When can I go home?

"Boy! This museum really needs two people to man the front! Maybe three!" I said as I collapsed in my chair.

Pat said, "There are work study students coming in to interview tomorrow morning. You'll need to hire at least three."

"I'll need to hire?" I asked.

"Yes, Caro. I'm quitting."

Twelve

"She's leaving in two weeks!" I exclaimed as I stirred ziti with one hand and chugged white wine with the other. "I was hired under false pretenses! Everyone knew Pat was leaving to work at the St. Martin's Shelter for the homeless! I should have gotten a clue the way she gave a bum some money! I don't want to work full time! I don't know what to do!"

"Quit now," John said. "Before it's too late."

"Why don't you wait and see, Mom," Max said. Naturally he'd like me to be gone all day, I thought.

Douglas said, "I can go to the university free if you work full time."

"There's that," John said.

"Oh I don't know why my life can't be normal!" I cried.

"Why be normal, Mom?" Max said.

***

I parked my car on a Walgreen's side street and walked to work the next day with great resolve. I will be nice during the interviews for student help. Then I will put in my resignation. I did not blame Pat for moving on with her life. I did hold the museum staff totally responsible for this deception. They can just have young people at the front desk and like it. And try to find some other idiot to manage their entire operation while they were sealed away doing God knows what.

Seven students were scheduled in the morning. Each one was very excited to be considered for a job in a museum. Pat sat and listened as I talked to an applicant. I had never done this before, but I really enjoyed the process. The young, the young...they possessed such energy and optimism. I felt uplifted chatting with such hopeful people. When the interviews were finished, I discussed my choices with Pat and she agreed. I offered the 20 hour a week job to a male pre-med student and two females, a flamenco dance major and an English major. They all accepted. I had to run a security check on them. I called the campus police with their vital information, and they told me clearance would take a week. Pat would still be here in the afternoons. I was done but surprisingly found myself thinking about how pleasant it could be working with happy people.

But instead of going home at 1:00, I marched down the hall to the powers that be to tell them I was quitting. I saw my very bad Inspector coming towards me.

"Oh! Hello," I said stupidly.

"Mrs. Steele," James said. "Can you please help me get to the handicapped lift in the basement? I'm quite turned around."

And I'm quite ready to explode, I thought.

"Of course! This building is like a rat's maze. Let's take the elevator down. Follow me, Inspector," I said briskly.

"I will."

"I found out some information about the murder victim." I said like a Miss Prim or Miss Priss.

"Oh did you now?"

"Well, yes I did, actually!" We stood in front of the elevator. I pressed the down button. "He used to teach in the Art Department. He taught me Contemporary Art ten years ago."

The doors opened. "I know," James said as he put his hand lightly on my waist so I stepped in first.

"But did you know why he was fired?" I pushed the basement button. The doors closed. His hand was still on my waist.

"Yes," James said.

"But did you know Roland was on the com…" James drew me close and kissed me. I pushed him away. I was terrified of my feelings, old school guilt and losing control. "I'm married!" I said.

"So am I."

I threw my purse on the floor, wrapped my arms around his neck and grabbed his beautiful hair. "I don't care. Kiss me again."

Thirteen

"Hate this!" I screamed as I threw another skirt on the bed. I was in my closet violently yanking clothes off their hangers. "Tacky! Tired!" I threw a peasant blouse through the air. "And shoes to match!" A pair of Birkenstocks flew across the room. My dog ran out. "Old! Ugly!" Stringy, stretched out sweaters sailed through the air. 94 Rock blared on the clock radio. Lamb of God was screeching *Walk With Me in Hell.* I shouted, "I'm probably going to wear these damn clothes in Hell! Horrible, most horrible!" I squeezed a limp polyester dress into a ball. "Damn Target cheap ass clothes!" I drop kicked a shiny black pencil skirt with the tags still on it in a high arc over the bed. "No, no, no, never, not ever in a million years...!" I pulled purses off the closet shelves and threw each of them backwards over my head. They bounced over the carpet. "What altered state was I in when I bought this shit!" I burst into tears and collapsed on the pile of discarded clothes. "What's wrong with me?" I wailed. I hugged an old blazer with huge shoulder pads. I stuffed a pillow between my legs and curled up in a fetal position. I remembered James's body pressed into mine and mine pressed into his. Against the elevator wall. His kiss. The way he touched me. The way I clung to him.

"Mom! What are you doing?" Max stood at the bedroom door.

"I'm thinking," I said sitting up. "School out this early?"

Max ignored the question. "Cleaning out your closet? Radical. Can I take these clothes to Buffalo Exchange? Can I keep the money? Do you like Lamb of God? What's for dinner?"

I threw a moth-eaten sweater at him. Max caught it, sat beside me, and held my hand. "This music depresses me, too," he said.

Fourteen

Since John was working late again, I just made French toast and bacon for dinner. The sweet maple syrup calmed me down a little. I ran a bath for hydrotherapy. But the comfort was short-lived. I started to get very hot even though the bath water cooled. "God! Am I running a fever?" My entire body was pounding. I felt like I was going to spontaneously combust. I had to get real.

I lay back into the fragrant bubbles and decided to revisit what happened with James logically. No tears, thrown clothes, or squeezing pillows between my legs. OK. I did not do anything wrong! I was not unfaithful! One very passionate, perfect kiss. Some delicious full body contact. A moment, that's all. Seconds, actually. No harm done. We stepped apart when the elevator landed on the basement floor. The door opened. Some students carrying guitar cases waited to get in. James picked up my purse and draped the strap gently over my shoulder. The young people stared. We walked out down the hall. My legs shook, but I carried on. Roland was waiting at the door to the handicapped lift. "I got your message, Inspector. Waited for you at my office. Our little Caro must have gotten a hold of you first! Ha!" (He's such a jerk, I thought as I sunk lower into the tub.)

"Mrs. Steele has been extremely helpful," James told him. Then he turned to me and said "thank you".

I said "you're welcome". I looked a Roland then said "I'm here to help". I could not meet James's green eyes. The end. Finished. I went back to work. I went home. I cleaned out my closet. How sane can one get?

The fever broke. Sweat poured out of me. This was a very strange sensation. My skin was wet in the bath water, but moisture was coming out of my body. I felt cleansed. But weak. I dried off, put on boxer shorts and tee shirt, got into bed with the dog and read a library book. No *A Cinnamon Summer* for me tonight. After a minute I threw down *Tales of the City*. How dare James kiss me! Not to mention the bite at the duck pond! He's married! He's being a bad boy! Who knows how many other women he's bitten. Or men, for that matter! I know nothing about him. What does he want from me? What do I want from him? I'm usually so careful around people. I fear losing control. I have no business starting an affair. I don't know how to act. All this time I had fantasized about James. I imagined. He was only in my head. The real, passionate contact horrified as well as thrilled me. Was this lust or love?

Did it matter? Did I really want to cross the line into adultery? God that sounded so Victorian. Did I want to leave my comfortable existence only to experience more erotic explosions? And that was just with one kiss! All right…two. I had never felt that way in my life. How long could those feelings last? I might like to know.

John came home around ten. "What's this?" He looked over the piles of clothes, purses and shoes stacked high against four walls. "What have you done?"

"I cleaned out my closet. Don't worry. Max will bring all of this to Buffalo Exchange tomorrow."

"I could get a tax write off if we donated to Retarded Citizens."

"You can't call them that anymore."

"ARCA! Stands for Association for Retarded Citizens, Caro!"

"Whatever!" I said and rubbed my dog's stomach. She flipped over so I could stroke every inch. But her ears were flat back against her head while we argued.

"What's wrong with you?" He picked up a dress with tags on it and waved it at me. "You haven't even worn this! You are so nervous! It's working at that damn university again! I don't like it. We don't need the money!"

"I feel fine. And I feel useful. It's different."

"We need you here."

"I am here!"

"Physically! But your mind must be somewhere else! Not with me, that's for sure. I guess I'm just a paycheck to you."

"And I'm just your brood mare and built-in maid." God, look at the Drama Queen! "You can be focused on work five days a week, but I can't focus on a life outside this house? I have needs and desires beyond you and the boys! It's not all about you!"

John threw up his hands. "Sorry I can't fulfill all of your needs."

"Sorry I can't fulfill all of yours, either!"

"You are restless." John kicked a pile of shoes. "And I'm hungry. Any leftovers?"

"No. I made breakfast for dinner. Why are you working late? It's not tax season."

"I have many clients who have needs outside of tax season," John said.

"Don't we all?"

"You know I don't like breakfast for dinner," he grumbled as walked out of the bedroom.

"Sad," I said.

John shut the door.

I sank into the pillows, pressed the back of my hand against my lips, and revisited, illogically, the pleasure of losing myself with James.

Fifteen

The student workers were a delight. Each one was a bright presence sitting at the front desk of the art museum. They were very engaging and polite with the public. The occasional odd character was treated with respect and some humor. Oh to be young and enthusiastic! I was proud of my choices. No one in the art museum administration commented on the youthful workers, although Linda asked me in a snarky way if I'd held auditions for the positions.

"Haha! You're funny, Linda." I had to admit they were a handsome group.

"Just so they do their job," Linda said over her shoulder as she lumbered out.

Oh just go back to your dungeon, I thought. You're scaring people away from here.

When I didn't have to greet every visitor and answer every phone call for seven people, I had time to look through catalogs for merchandise to sell in the gift shop. Today flamenco dancer Cathy was sitting at the front. I sat behind the desk in a corner like Pam did when she was training me. As I flipped through pages, I kept looking up at every one who walked through the Center for the Arts foyer. If I saw James again, I did not know what I planned to say. Maybe nothing. Seemed to work well last time. What if he called me? He should call me! After what happened any gentleman should call. But am I a lady? I still will not know what to say. I decided that here is now, the past is the past, and no one knows the future. So I tore my eyes away from the foyer to study pages of art cards.

"Is my precious Pat gone already?" I heard a gravelly lisp and smelled booze and BO.

"Pat works this afternoon," Cathy said politely. "Can I help you?"

"Leroy needs a few dollars," Leroy said.

"Well, I…," Cathy began and looked at me in a panic. I stood up.

"Leroy! Hello! Pat will be here later."

"Ahhhh. Pleeeze. A little something…doesn't have to be much." He started to walk around the desk towards me.

"We do not give money," I said, stood up, and blocked his way around the desk. I noticed the Satellite Coffee Shop kiosk was setting up in the foyer for the Albuquerque Public School sponsored musical matinee of *Annie* in Popejoy Hall. "But I will buy you a cup of coffee."

"Ahhhh. Come on." Leroy whined.

"And a cookie."

"Oh all right."

I told Cathy to text me if she needed assistance. She told me to have fun. Leroy shuffled behind me as we walked across the foyer to the Satellite counter. This could be a perfect opportunity to get some information, I thought. I wanted to know more about Charlie. I hoped Leroy still had a memory. Leroy sat down on a bench along the wall while I bought him a regular coffee and soft-baked chocolate chip cookie.

"What? No Cinnamon Dolce Frappuccino?" Saliva sprayed out of his mouth.

"Hahaha, Leroy."

He winked at me, took a slurp of coffee and tore off half the cookie. I sat next to him in a friendly way. I listened to him gum the cookie and growl 'mmm' with his mouth full.

"So, terrible about Charlie's death. Pat told me that you knew him," I said. "I had him for a class years ago. He was an excellent teacher."

"Yeah he was a good teacher! And a good friend! Had bad luck that Charlie."

"How so?"

"The man was set up! He never touched those girls! Or harassed them!"

"Why did they make those accusations then? What motive did they have?"

"That son of a bitch Roland put them up to it. Probably paid them! He's filthy rich. He doesn't need to work. He doesn't work! Asshole! And those whores left before finishing the semester. What does that tell you?"

People started to stare. Children were lining up to get into Popejoy Hall. Chaperones gave us dirty looks. "Please lower your voice, Leroy," I whispered.

"Roland wanted to get rid of Charlie from the time he became the big shot Art Museum director. Which by the way should be called the Anthropology Museum. So much old shit in there. Charlie should have been director. What an artist. A true artist. One of a kind. I miss him. He was my friend..." Leroy started crying.

I took his empty cup and threw it away. I got Satellite napkins. I came back, handed him napkins and patted his back. He blew his nose and wiped his eyes.

"Of course you miss your friend," I said. "Why did Roland hate Charlie?"

"Oh that's a story. Are you ready, little missy, to hear a tale to try men's souls? And women's?"

"I am."

"When the university fired Charlie, and he moved to El Morro, Roland's wife went with him."

"What?"

"Oh yes."

"Did Roland know his wife was seeing Charlie?"

"He didn't have a clue. Heh heh. Charlie loved Anne. I told him to watch out. The affair could come to no good in this incestuous rat's nest of a college. But he didn't listen." Leroy picked cookie crumbs off his jacket and inhaled them.

"Where is Anne now?"

"Anne left Charlie after a year in El Morro. She went

back to Maine. Charlie told me the isolation drove her crazy. She probably was already crazed married to Roland for so many years. But Charlie was devastated. Then there was the fire. He went downhill from there."

"But Roland is married now."

"Yeah. He divorced Anne and found someone else right away. He has money. Quite a catch for certain females. He married a woman named Olive who rides her bike and collects dolls."

Well, Roland may have remarried but still could hate Charlie intensely for being with his first wife. Bruised ego. Power plays. Destroying a life. I could see it all happening.

Pat did not tell me this. Leroy got up. "I need a drink," he said. "Can you give me a little something?"

"No, but thank you for talking to me. I am sorry for the loss of your friend. I have to go back to the museum." I stood up and lightly put my hand on his arm. "But one more thing, Leroy. Do you know the names of the girls who accused Charlie of harassment?"

"Ah." Leroy scratched his wispy hair. Flakes of dandruff floated down and coated his shabby military jacket. "Something like a flower--Daisy, Petal, Belladonna, Holly--but I heard they got a job right away working at an upscale gallery in Nob Hill. Attached at the hip, those females. Working in concert to wreck lives."

"Could you describe them?"

"Tiny skinny bitches. Sharp teeth. Purple hair."

"Gee thanks. "

Leroy looked at me a long time. I briefly saw an intelligent spark in his eyes. "You are not like Pat. You are different. I will come back." He lurched through the foyer out the front doors.

Chapter 16

Cathy's shift was over. Mike, the pre-med student, came in. A huge group of people arrived from Family, Youth, and Development. One girl was in a wheelchair. I told Mike that I could take her around to the back door of the Museum. Pat was not here yet. Mike could corral the kiddies stampeding and yelling down the steps into the main gallery.

"Please no running in the art museum!" Mike said in a deep voice. The supervisors looked dazed. Why don't the adults give a talk on proper behavior before visiting a museum? Like being quiet in a library? Watching a movie? A play? Basic civility.

I pushed the young girl out the main door, down the hall, and to the elevator. We rolled in and pressed the Ground Floor. Her name was Celeste. She was very excited to come to the university. I looked at the wall of infamy and imagined myself pressed against it against

James's body. We shuddered to a stop. I wheeled her to the back door, unlocked it, and entered the main gallery.

"Let someone at the front desk know when you are ready to go to the lower gallery."

"Thank you, Ma'am." Celeste said. Civility was not dead after all.

When I got back to the main desk Pat was there.

"You can go now, Caro! Sorry I was late. Could not find a parking place."

"Can I talk to you for a minute?" I asked.

Pat looked around the museum. The rowdy group had calmed down. Mike was standing up with his arms crossed watching over them. "Looks like Mike has things in control," she said. Mike gave her a thumbs up. We walked into the foyer.

"I had a talk with Leroy this morning," I said.

"Oh did he bother you? I am so sorry! I have set a bad precedent. You do not need this distraction!" Pat said.

"No, it's not that," I said. "He told me that Roland's first wife ran away with Charlie."

"What?"

"Yes! Is this an alcoholic man's hallucination or true?"

"I don't know, Caro. I do know that he married Olive shortly after accepting the position of director here. I haven't heard anything else."

"Why did Leroy know? Surely word would have gotten all around the College of Fine Arts!"

"I heard nothing, Caro. Maybe this is all in Leroy's imagination. He hates Roland intensely. He may have made this up out of grief for losing Charlie. Blaming Roland makes sense to his alcoholic mind."

"Anne supposedly moved back to Maine. Someone should contact her."

"Oh Caro! You are such an investigator! Why don't you call that inspector...what's his name?"

"James Hutchinson."

"Yes, Inspector Hutchinson. He is the one you should talk to."

"Thanks. What a good suggestion."

Seventeen

I got my purse out of the back closet. I left the Center for the Arts for the long walk to my car. I remembered that I had to stop at Sprouts on the way home for a fucking chicken for dinner. I did not notice James standing by the sculpture of two flamenco dancers until he touched my elbow. I turned around and almost fainted. I must have stumbled, because he put his arm through mine. I leaned into his side and froze.

"Can we talk?" he asked.

I nodded. We walked arm and arm to the short, concrete raised border of the sloping grass expanse in front of the Center. We sat on its smooth, flat surface. He took my hand.

"Are you all right?" James asked.

I nodded.

"About what happened yesterday. My actions may have…"

"Please," I said. "I...I...it's OK."

"You hung on good." James slowly unfolded each of my fingers and gently kissed the palm of my hand.

"No bites?" I asked.

"Maybe later," he said.

"In your dreams. Now I have news for you." James started to rub his finger very lightly up and down the inside of my wrist. "Don't distract me from the facts." But I felt chills in every inch of my body and did not pull away. "Do you want to know what I know or not?"

"I always want to know what you know."

"Roland's first wife ran away with Charlie, the murdered homeless man."

James dropped my hand to whip out his notebook and pen. "What?"

"Leroy told me."

"Who's Leroy?"

"A homeless man who roams around the Fine Arts Center. He was Charlie's best friend. Leroy was fired from the Art Faculty and so was Charlie. Roland was on the Academic Committee who voted on both cases. I was going to tell you this yesterday, but…"

"What's Leroy's last name?"

"I don't know. You can probably find out from the Art Department. I can call."

"What's Roland's ex-wife's name?"

"Anne. I don't know if she kept her married name Walters. She's in Maine now. I think someone should contact her. But can you trust Leroy? He drinks. Pat, who has worked here a long time never heard this story, so I don't know if it's true or an alcoholic's delusion…"

James stood up. "Excellent work, Mrs. Steele."

"I'm MRS. STEELE now?" I exclaimed.

James put the notebook and pen in his jacket pocket. He pulled me close. I wrapped my arms around his waist. Our noses almost touched. He was going to kiss me. I didn't care. I saw my Vogue sunglasses reflected in his Ray Bans.

"You will always be Mrs. Steele to me," James said. He left to walk quickly toward Central Avenue talking on his cell phone.

I watched him unable to move. Then I had a hot flash. My gums started tingling. I had to sit down. Immediately. My body was taking over my brain. Reasonable thought vanquished. No standing back for mind control. What a strange, foreign, scary feeling. I liked it. A lot. I may run amok. The possibilities made my knees go weak.

Eighteen

"What a cozy scene."

I whirled around to see Linda standing there holding a 32 oz. container of soda and a huge Chick-fil-A bag.

I stood up, gave her a closed mouth smile, turned, and walked away. None of her business how cozy I got.

"I think you might like to know that Pat is not leaving after all."

Well, that got my attention! I stopped and faced the gorgon.

"The Art Museum is leasing the Graham Gallery downtown to be our satellite museum. Pat will manage it. It will only be open part of the day so she can zip over a few blocks to St. Martin's and work with the homeless."

"I'm happy to hear that Pat will still be on the staff."

"Thought you would be, Caro. We want you to bring some shop merchandise down there. And some books to sell. OK?"

"OK."

Linda gave me a smirk and lumbered away.

God she bugged me. But she was kind to tell me the news. I was so relieved. I could see Pat. And hopefully get more information about Art Museum politics. I was afraid, however, that the truth was as sealed off and hidden like all of the administrative staff combined. But we shall see what we shall see, my mother used to say.

***

I decided to go to La Montanita Coop grocery store in Nob Hill to get the fucking chicken. They only carried what I called "happy" chickens raised on Rosie's Farm in Los Lunas, NM. They died happy. Until they got their heads chopped off, they got to run free over a grassy range, peck unmodified corn and seeds, and snatch organic (I'm sure!) insects, flies, snails, and worms. They had such fun for a while. Expensive little piece of fowl but our family could afford it, I rationalized, waiting in the checkout line as I mentally clicked off all the galleries I knew of in Nob Hill. Of course I forgot my reusable grocery bag, got the obligatory sad look and tilt of the head from the checker. I had to get home and eat something. I will go gallery trolling later.

When I got home I saw that I had a message from Tina. She was probably anxious to know how I liked her new novel. I barely started it. I will call her after I eat and read a little more *Cinnamon Summer*. Tina worked so hard on her writing every day. I respected that. I will respond. But first a fried egg sandwich and 5,000 Doritos. I sat in bed, ate my lunch while hunched over the manuscript. Where was I? Oh yeah…Lily was hungry. I read:

Fortified by the slice of cheese pizza, salad, and pink lemonade, Lily drove the rest of the way to Greenport.

She pulled up in front of her aunt's house. She checked her hair and eye-make-up in the mirror. Reaching in her near-by polka-dot make-up bag, she reapplied her Silver Jonquil lipstick, wiped the tear stained mascara from under her eyes with tissue, and spritzed her face with Lancome Tonique Douceur.

(I used those products! And wear Havaianas! Was Tina raining on my parade? Oh! Maybe someday I will write a novel instead of taking torture jobs!)

She licked her fingers and ran them over her eyebrows. After adjusting her pink floral wrap blouse and brushing the dog hair off her navy culottes, Lily got out of the car. Tulip jumped after her. She knocked on the door. No answer. Hmm. She knocked again louder. Maybe Aunt Geneva was going deaf.

She turned around suddenly when she heard vicious barking and growling. She saw her precious boxer rolled over on her back in the grass. Standing over her gnashing its teeth and frothing at the mouth, was a huge black and tan Rottweiler. "Get away, you brute!" Lily threw her African woven purse at the attacking dog.

(I have an African bag!!! This is getting ridiculous!)

"Bruno, Come!" a voice shouted from the back yard. The drooling dog ran off. Tulip stood up and shook

herself. Lily checked her all over. No blood. Oh! What a welcome!

"Who are you?" A deep voice voice hollered.

Lily tore her eyes away from Tulip to see a man dressed in cut-offs and a wife beater tee. His thick blonde hair was pulled back in a pony tail. His eyes covered by the blackest Ray-Bans. He had a wide chiseled mouth. He wore black high-top Chuck Taylor All Star Converse sneakers without socks. He was about 6 feet tall with a slender, firm build. He must play baseball or tennis, Lily thought all in a matter of seconds. He held a rake. His rude dog wagged its tail by his side.

"Well? Cat got your tongue?" The stranger walked closer to her, invading her personal space. Lily could smell clean sweat and freshly mown grass. His teeth were so white.

Lily stood up to her full 5'6". "My name is Lily Bartlett. I have driven all the way from Texas. My Aunt Geneva lives here. I am going to stay--"

"Your cottage isn't ready yet. Come back later." He spun around and walked behind the house. Lily stared at his back open-mouthed. Bruno scampered after him. And Tulip pranced behind both of them. My little girl has no shame, Lily thought!

"Where's my Aunt?" Lily yelled up in the air.

"Riding the Carousel!"

"What?"

No reply.

"Tulip!" Lily called her dog. "Let's go bye-bye in the car car!" No response. Lily marched around her Aunt's house. The backyard looked like an advertisement for a

Master Gardener Handbook : Flower beds, a gazebo, lush thick dark green grass, raspberry bushes, and a flagstone path that wound around a small pond with water lilies and ended at the steps of a small, white shingled cottage. Did this brute create such a paradise? Inconceivable!!! Both dogs were stretched out on the lawn. "Tulip! Come on!" *Tulip raised her head, twitched her ears, and lay back down next to Bruno.* "Do I have to get the leash?"

"Oh for crying out loud let her stay here. She's been cooped up in a car!" *The man knelt down and stroked her ears. Tulip lazily wagged her cropped tail while Bruno licked her paw.*

"What's your name?" *Lily asked him.*

He stood and took off his sunglasses. "Chance. Chance Nail."

His piercing aquamarine eyes shot through her like a laser beam. She felt an odd, delicious twitch between her legs and flushed red hot.

"Well, thank you for watching my dog, Chance."

(What? Chance Nail??? Sounds like a stage name for a porno star. Oh Tina! Where are you going with this story?)

There was one main road in Greenport. Two stop lights. Quaint residential side streets branched off from it. The bay was on the east side of the hamlet. One could see it from the main road. There was a dock and boats and two piers. Lily thought she saw an old-fashioned Carousel between the piers when she first drove in. She came to Main Street passing charming white homes with porches, flags, and twirly-gigs hanging from roofs. Many yards had cute trolls and gnomes. The streets were so clean! Lily got a little chill thinking this was like Stepford Town, but then remembered that Chance was here with his dog and they were not perfect! No, not by a long shot!

(Chance surely had some perfect qualities.)

But she wondered about that unusual tremor she'd had between her legs. Where did that come from? Too many hours driving in Gap bikini cotton panties? And why did she get so hot?

(You had *la petite mort*, you silly *canard*! Probably the first.)

She saw the Carousel set back from the street in the middle of a meadow. It looked like something out of a movie. It was huge and covered on top like a majestic circus tent complete with a red flag on the swirled top. The sides of the Carousel were encircled by diagonal openings so one could see the colorful, painted horses, dragons, and magical creatures going around and around and up and down. Organ music played A Hot Time in the Old Time Tonight. Where was her Aunt Geneva? Lily walked up closer. A red head flew by on a unicorn with her legs held high in the air.

Well! Geneva! Finally an interesting character, I thought as I closed the manuscript. I looked forward to Chance Nail shaking Lily's world. Ah. Romance. Soft porn. I day dreamed about James's mouth and fell asleep. Suki's barking woke me up.

I stumbled into the living room. Douglas stood there with a very pretty girl. He introduced Megan to me and said she played the flute in their school marching band. They had to study. I said "Oh where? The library?"

"Oh no! My room!"

"Oh. Really. Do you want something to eat or drink?"

"No, we're fine!" They both went down the hall laughing and slammed the bedroom door. Raucous electronic music started. How can anyone study with that noise? Growing up I never could have a boy in my room with the door closed. Oh the young, the young.

Max came out of his room.

"When did you get home?" I demanded.

"A while ago." Max tiptoed to his older brother's closed door. He put a finger to his lips and his ear on the door. We both listened to the throbbing music, shrill giggles and low-pitched chuckles. Max looked at me, frowned and shook his head.

"Doesn't sound good, Mom," he whispered gravely. "May I suggest--"

"Never mind, you!" I turned and stomped into the kitchen.

Max followed. "What's wrong, Mom?"

"I don't know what to do with this happy chicken."

"Don't worry about it! You have to start having fun, Mom! You work too much! You are taking care of everyone except yourself." Max took a lemon and orange out of the refrigerator. He pulled a carton of salt out of the cupboard and a large pot from under the counter. He yanked a knife out of a drawer. He hacked the orange in half. "Look. I'll squeeze this orange over the happy bird, rub it with Kosher salt, stuff a lemon up its butt and throw it in the oven."

"Where did you learn that?"

"Recipe in *The Albuquerque Journal: Pollo Feliz con Naranja y Limon.* I do read more than ads."

I hugged my tall baby. "You just made that up!"

Max hugged me back. "Have some fun, Mom."

Out of the mouths of babes. Such wisdom. I have to start doing something to make me forget everything in my life. Submerge myself in oblivion. I will seek water.

Nineteen

Pat arrived for her afternoon shift. Cathy left and Alana came to work. I hugged Pat.

"Linda told me you were staying on staff! I was so happy to hear that, Pat! Even if you will be all the way down Central from me!"

"Thank you, Caro. I think this is best for now. St. Martin's could only offer me a part-time social worker position at this time. And I really need full-time work. So you can't get rid of me."

"As if I ever wanted to!"

"You'll still have to work more hours since I won't be here in the afternoons."

"I know. I'm trying to work out schedules with my husband and kids."

"Let them start doing more around the house!"

"Yea...have to start cracking the whip."

"And the Graduate Student Art Exhibit is going

up next week. They're hanging Friday through the weekend. Ken is taking down the main gallery show Thursday, but the lower gallery will keep the current exhibits. Just a reminder that we'll be closed Sunday and of course Monday. Then the Grand Opening is Tuesday at 5:30.

"What do I have to do now?"

"Nothing! Brenda, our publicity coordinator, has catered food from the sub and hired the UNM Jazz Band. You and your crew have to maintain order. No making out in the lower gallery! No food or drink splashed on the art! You really have to start attending the weekly staff meetings. I won't be able to do those anymore."

"Oh goody. Something to look forward to."

We watched a group of elderly people come in. They were physically fit and could navigate the stairs. They greeted us loudly. Too loudly. They were a happy group. Just glad to be here.

"Manzano Del Sol Alzheimer unit," Pat whispered.

All of a sudden we heard whoops and hollers! They were pointing to the Spanish Colonial painting of St. Lawrence roasting on a grill. I found their vocal outbursts very satisfying unlike unruly young people. They were expressing delight or horror. Art was affecting them which art should do. Other visitors did give them a wide berth. But too bad.

"You are way past your shift, Caro," Pat said. "You should go home for lunch and a few hours of quiet."

"Oh I am trying a new routine. I already ate some yogurt, a Kind bar, and an apple at morning break. I am going to swim a few days a week. I mean Johnson Center is right across from the Fine Arts Center. I need to lose weight. And swimming used to make me feel so good."

"It's a beautiful pool. Have fun!"

I picked up my purse and Virgin of Guadalupe oilskin bag of swim gear out of the back closet, marched out of the museum, across the foyer, out the door, past the Fiesta dancers, and up the steps into Johnson Center. I swiped my UNM ID through the turnstile strip, and pushed through.

I had not been to the UNM pool since my children were young. We used to go every afternoon during the summer. I always felt they were safe either in the Olympic Pool or the Therapeutic Pool while I swam laps. Outside was soft, lush grass where I would lie out on a towel, look at the sky and daydream.

I had to read the signs for directions to the women's locker room. I walked up and down a lot of ramps and corridors. Many renovations changed Johnson Gym into Johnson Center. I finally found a very large, clean locker room. Pulled on my ten year old Costco bathing suit, took a brief shower, glanced at myself in a mirror--gads. Note to get my varicose veins removed!

Now I had to find the pool. More signs, more ramps, then the double doors, the chlorine smell, the echoes, the splashes, water. The indoor Olympic Pool was huge--long enough for canoe and kayaking classes and deep enough for scuba diving instruction. On each side of the building glass doors leading out to grassy grounds lined ¾ of the length of the building. Natural light poured in. I put my bag of personal items and towel on a bench next to an empty lap lane. I took a deep breath. I dove in. What a rush. I loved it.

So two laps of crawl, two laps of side stroke, two laps of breast stroke, two laps of back stroke. Enough of that. Now for some lolling around in the water: dead man floats, swimming like a mermaid, doing somersaults.... I had to leave the lap lane and get over to the open swimming section of the pool. I did not feel like hoisting myself up and walking over past only two lap lanes. I checked to see when the other lap swimmers were down at the other end, and quickly dove under water through two lanes toward the shallower section. My feet touched the bottom. I bounced up for air. I came down right in front of my Inspector.

Twenty

"You!" I sputtered and went back under. His grabbed me under my armpits and lifted me up.

"Hello, Mrs. Steele," he said.

"What are you doing here?" I put my hands on his shoulders and shook my head like a dog.

"I'm swimming." James started walking backwards. I hung on. Floating.

"Don't the police have their own pool?"

"Why yes…but I have a temporary pass to use Johnson Center since I am working on campus."

"How nice." I loved floating holding on to James.

"It's become even nicer," he said.

"Oh yes. Very nice." I floated.

"I saw you walk in and watched you swim."

"Really, now."

"You're very good." He walked in circles. I swished around.

"I used to be a lifeguard," I said.

"Really, now."

"So you swim, huh?" I asked like an idiot.

"Indeed I do. About a mile."

"That is so good for you."

James stopped moving and said, "One of the things that's so good for me, Mrs. Steele."

I looked dreamily into his eyes. I started blinking. James got blurry. I suddenly realized how I must look. I never wore goggles because they smother me, so my eyes were burning from chlorine and certainly bloodshot. I never wore a swimming cap because they tortured me, so my hair was plastered to my head. What a sight! I let go of James and dog paddled to the edge of the pool where I held on and slowly kicked my feet. James glided up next to me. He turned on his stomach and held on to the edge. We kicked our feet lazily and stared at each other for a long time. I wanted to ask him about his marriage. But I was afraid to. I did not want to think about it. I did not want to think about my marriage, either. I did not want to ruin the magical feeling I had submerged in water so close to him. As the Yogis say: Here is now. So instead I rubbed my eyes so I could clearly see his entire self in a bathing suit. Thank goodness no muscle bound Atlas. But I had already sensed that. I bet he used to play baseball. No visible tattoos. A few freckles. Manly hair on forearms. Not too much on the chest. No spandex bikini. Honest boxer shorts. Honest everything. I was dying. James was really looking at me, too. I didn't want him to notice my ugly feet. I distracted him with the case.

"So how is the investigation going?"

"I cannot say."

"Well, I will say then! Roland seems to be a prime suspect."

"He was in Kansas City playing poker that night."

"What?"

"His poker club took the Amtrak to Kansas City for barbeque and a card game."

"What a bunch of fun guys."

"They all were actually. Very entertaining interviews."

I was turning into a prune. I pressed my feet up against the side of the pool. I pushed back suddenly, flipped over and swam underwater until James caught my ankle. I surfaced. He let go, grabbed me around the waist and crushed me to him. I shrieked and wrapped myself around his body. The lifeguard blew her whistle.

Twenty One

"Well, what happened next?" my sister asked.

"Oh nothing. We flew apart and started laughing. We swam to the steps at the end of the pool and got out. He walked me to the bench where my bags were. Then we went out the doors to the lockers. He kissed my hand. He went his way. I went mine. The end. Of the report." I sighed.

We sipped our martinis. Sally and I were sitting in the window of the bar at Scalo Northern Italian Grill in Nob Hill.

"God knows what might have happened," she said and speared a piece of calamari and dipped it in marinara sauce and aioli.

"I'm sure! We were in the open swim area! Kids were whacking each other with pool noodles. Mothers dunking their babies up and down." I pushed the squiggly pieces of calamari toward my sister. They looked too much like sea creatures. I didn't want to know what I was eating. "He's playing with me, Sally."

"You're playing with him, too, sister!"

"He's like a drug. I can't get enough of him. It's like I'm on fire."

"You're playing with fire."

"Then I'll burn in Hell."

"Cute. Listen to me. You are attracted to him. Nothing wrong with that. You're human! You haven't done anything...yet. Accept these feelings. But also be aware that you do not know this man. He said he was married. He has been back to New Orleans doing God knows what in that city with God knows who. Does he have children? Does he have friends? Have you met them?"

"I know...I know..."

"This is sounding very much like a teenage crush. And you are miles away from that age bracket. And you have three wonderful sons. And a husband who loves you..."

"I am thankful for my children..."

"Are you going to risk all you have and all you've built and created for a virtual stranger who only gives you a fever? And nothing else?"

"But I like having a fever, Sally."

"Fevers eventually break. Or they kill you."

I looked at my sister. Unlike me, a child bride and mother, she had wild times before she married in her 30s. She had lots of boyfriends. She hitchhiked a year across Europe with a girlfriend. I bet her temperature spiked more than once over the years. (While mine stayed at

98.6 for decades.) Childless, I often thought that she needed my family to feel complete. Our mother had died twenty years before, and our Dad had remarried. Our brother was dead. I was the stability in her life. She did not want to lose that. Oh my imagination was running wild. Why couldn't I accept people's love and advice? And not think they had a hidden agenda. I took a deep breath, squeezed her hand and smiled.

"Want to check out Mariposa Gallery?"

"Why?"

"Oh…I heard they had a new owner since they relocated here from Old Town. Just want to see their place, that's all."

"Hmmmm. You have a gleam in your eye. Like you're on a mission. And you have changed the subject!"

We paid our bill and left the bar. As we walked outside past Scalo's long glass windows facing Central Avenue, I saw John sitting at a table with Alice, his secretary. He was talking. She was dipping bread in olive oil. I grabbed Sally's arm as she reached in her purse for sunglasses.

"You have gotten so weird," she said as I yanked her along.

Twenty Two

I will think about John later, I thought, as pushed the doors to Mariposa Gallery open. Now I have to focus and keep my eyes peeled for tiny girls with sharp teeth.

What an explosion of color and design in perfect display. Everywhere one looked there were exquisite, whimsical, beautiful, and grotesque works of art. And that was not counting the jewelry arranged in a case that circled the middle of the gallery. And there was an upstairs. And puppets, flying beasties and fairies dangled from the ceiling. What a place! I'd love to work here.

"May I help you?" A tall, slender middle-aged woman in a black, silky jumpsuit walked up to us. Her white hair was coiled in a French roll. She had on a hint of lipstick and light violet smudges around her hazel eyes. Her nails were short and ox blood red. She wore a huge skull ring on her right hand. Ruby shards glistened in the eye sockets. On her beautiful feet were black Greek sandals. Huge silver hoops hung from her ears. I did not know what my sister was thinking, but I suddenly felt as if I had been digging in the dirt with sticks while I stood next to this living work of art. I realized I often had the feeling that I looked like a scumbag shopping in most Nob Hill stores. Like I had to get really dressed up to even buy coffee beans. Oh I had to get over myself and get down to business.

"We're just looking, thank you!" I purred.

"Well, my name is Olive if you need anything," she purred back and walked behind the jewelry cases. Everyone's an actress.

"Let's go upstairs, Sally!" Once again I squeezed my claw around her arm and led her away.

"God! What's wrong with you?"

"Shh!" I hissed. Then said with great vocal enthusiasm: "I want to see the mixed media collection! I think Kyle Zimmerman is showing here."

Olive leaned over the display cases. "Indeed she is! Wonderful artist, photographer, and writer!"

"I know. She's a friend of mine," I smiled with a closed mouth and crinkled my eyes.

"You are so full of shit," Sally said as we got to the upper level.

"Well! Kyle's taken my head shot! She knows me!"

Kyle's work was magical and beautiful. Like stepping into world of swirling elements, fauna and living creatures. I felt like I had travelled to a mysterious destination after looking at her art. But enough of that…"Her name is Olive!" I whispered when we both were admiring a piece in a far corner.

"Her who?"

"The woman at the front of the gallery!" I said through clenched teeth.

"What am I supposed to do? Faint?"

"That's Roland Walters' wife's name!"

"Who?"

"Roland! The Art Museum Director!"

"You told me that she just rode her bike and played with dolls!" Sally put her glasses on to read a label on the wall.

"That's what Pat told me!"

"Maybe it's not the same Olive. There could be many Olives in Albuquerque."

"I don't think so." My sister and I whirled around. There was the one and only Olive. She must have followed us upstairs like a cat.

"I like to think I'm pretty unique in this town," she purred. Again. "And I do ride my bike for exercise. And my dolls love the new addition we built for them."

"Oh good!" I started babbling. "My name is Caro. This is my sister Sally. I just started working at the UNM Art Museum. I, of course, met your husband, Roland. I heard by the grapevine that he had a wife named Olive who cycled and collected lovely dolls."

"The grapevine, huh? Well, why don't you go back to the grapevine and tell them I have a new interest."

"I will certainly tell everyone I know that you are at Mariposa. And may I congratulate you on your new interest in this world-class gallery. Thank you for your hospitality!" I slipped my arm through my sister's. God help me I almost curtsied.

We started downstairs. We stepped aside to let a petite young woman going up pass. She was all in black. She had a tablet and pen. No purse. She must work here, I thought. Her hair was so black. Must be dyed. Nobody's hair is that black. She stopped when she was directly across from us.

"Please let me know if you need any help!" Her wide smile revealed sharp, tiny teeth.

"We will!" I crowed.

I stopped abruptly at the front display case to sign the guest book. I wrote down a fake e-mail address. I did not want Olive to be able to contact me. But she did know where I worked. Me and my big mouth. I took a few business cards. Olive materialized by my side with her arm around the young assistant's waist.

"Holly and I hope to see you, again, Caro," Olive said. "And your sister."

***

Sally and I walked to our cars parked behind the Nob Hill Shopping Center.

"Ok, I have to say it. I've never heard such a ration of shit. I have a new respect for your acting abilities," she said.

"Never mind theatre! I am talking life! I am on to something, Sally! Roland's wife and a sharp-toothed assistant in the same gallery? Too much of a coincidence! I can't wait to tell my Inspector!"

"Your Inspector? Oh Caro…what are you doing?"

"Everything. For once."

Twenty Three

I stretched out in bed. I felt so good after a hot bath. The sheets were cool. I had on freshly washed and softened boxer shorts and tee. Suki was curled up at the end of the bed. I tucked my feet under her warm body. I was reading *Pride and Prejudice* for the 109th time. I had information for my Inspector. The owner of Mariposa Gallery was married to Roland. And, most likely, the girls who brought charges against the murdered man Charlie were working for her. Life was good.

John came in and sat on the bed. Of course I had not said anything about seeing him with his secretary at Scalo. I often thought our marriage had lasted so long because we both suffered from conflict avoidance syndrome. And at this point I had my mind on other matters that excited me, and really did not care what John did.

"I don't feel like you care about me anymore," he began.

I looked at the clock. Ten-thirty. Perfect time to start a heavy conversation. I stared at him silently. I was not going to jump in and babble on to make him feel better. He can do the babbling.

He wasn't taking the bait. Silence. Hang dog look.

"Can I hold you?" he asked.

I nodded my head. He could get so pitiful. He was another child in the house.

Immediately I was in one of his bear hugs. John buried his head in my neck. Then he started wetly kissing my arms and breasts. And I had just bathed! Oh I was a frigid wife! What woman could refuse such expressive love? I guessed that woman was me. I patted his back. Suki jumped off the bed. John moved on top of me.

"The kids!" I exclaimed.

John got up, nudged the dog out of the bedroom, closed and locked the door.

"I'm really tired," I said. I did not want to have sex with him.

"I have missed you," he said.

"I am here!"

"Physically, but mentally and emotionally you are somewhere else. Come back to me!" John said. He fell on me.

He started to kiss me. His tongue went down my throat. I turned my head, pushed his chest and rolled out from under him. I stood up. "I'm not in the mood, John!"

"You are never in the mood anymore."

"Oh go have a pity party with Alice. If you haven't already."

"Fucking bitch!" John yelled. He stormed out and slammed the door. The front door opened and slammed shut. I heard his car peel out of the driveway. Good riddance! Fucking bastard! My heart was beating fast. My eyes filled with tears. I was mad! I was scared! My life as I knew it was falling apart.

I opened the bedroom door to look for Suki. She was under the coffee table in the living room. Douglas stepped out of his room in a blast of Black Keys music. Max appeared out of nowhere. My sons put their arms around me. I felt Suki's cold nose against my leg.

Twenty Four

I woke up alone. I finally got to sleep after drinking two glasses of wine and smoking on the deck. I had a headache. I sat up and recited my usual line from a psalm: This is the day that the Lord hath made. I will rejoice and be glad in it. Then I fell back, smashed a pillow over my face and realized my secure, stable home life was going to Hell. I rolled out of bed, threw on a sweatshirt and stumbled to the kitchen. What? No food odors greeted me. Usually Max created a unique combination of leftovers for breakfast. I only smelled coffee.

The early morning sun was blasting through the east kitchen window. I turned around to get my sunglasses off the living room bookshelf. I entered the kitchen once more. Max was sitting at the table slowly eating a bowl of Cheerios. *The Albuquerque Journal* lay unread on the table.

"What's wrong?" I asked.

"Nothing."

I filled a glass with orange juice and set it in front of him. "Are you sick?"

"No."

"Good." I kissed him on his head. No product. Just fluffy brown hair with red highlights. I put my lips on his forehead to check for a fever. Cool.

"Dad was here. He made coffee and left."

"Did he say anything?"

"No."

I got a coffee cup. As I poured I saw a note propped up by the canisters. Hmm. Later. I sat down at the kitchen table. I took off my shades. I put them on the table. I looked at Max.

Max put his spoon down on the table. He looked at me. Intense stare-down. "Is it that Inspector?" he asked.

"No," I lied.

"Whatever you say, Mom." He got up, put his bowl on the floor for Suki to lick and walked out. He came back, picked up the empty bowl and put it in the sink. He was definitely not himself today. "Douglas wanted me to tell you that he has jazz band practice after school."

"OK, but I'll see you after school, right?"

Max leaned over and put his arms around me. "Yes, you will, Mom." He left.

I started to cry. None of that. I couldn't have puffy eyes for work. My public! But tears rolled down my cheeks anyway in spite of me biting my tongue. I must move. I jumped up, grabbed the note, and went outside. What did that asshole have to say?

***

I drank coffee and stared at the Sandia Mountains. A sudden breeze blew the opened note off my lap. I watched the paper dance across the grass before sailing over the fence.

I hated it that John loved me so much.

I hated it that I lied to Max.

Twenty Five

When I got to work, the main gallery was bursting with the messy chaotic energy of youth, art, video, audio, and sculpture. The Juried Graduate Exhibition was going up. A real happening. Ken, the curator of exhibitions, was roaming around shaking his head. He looked like he was going to have a stroke. No one was listening to his expert advice. When he hung a show there was classical music playing. He had his leveler. He had his ladder. He had a hammer. The graduate students were mounting their work themselves. Running here and there asking for nails, band-aids, mechanical staplers, stools, and brooms. Some of the exhibits were truly exciting works of art while others included a chicken wire sculpture in the shape of a chicken, a room-sized square constructed in astro-turf with green tinsel hanging from the ceiling, a video of a volcano erupting to the music of Beethoven's 5th Symphony, a video loop

of a woman crying and laughing, and a wall of used tea bags. Cathy and I watched with great amusement. It was like performance art. The downstairs galleries were still open, so we welcomed visitors. They stopped and stared at the main gallery activity before going down the stairs.

The woman who was hanging tea bags approached Ken. He started waving his arms. She came over to the desk.

"Excuse me. Do you have any thumbtacks I could borrow? Ken got really upset when I asked him for some."

"I only have red push pins," I said.

"Oh! They'll do! Thanks!"

I still had a headache. Then I saw Leroy lurch in. He was all smiles.

"Finally this looks like a happy place!" he lisped. "How about a little something to help me celebrate this miraculous transformation?" He leaned way over the front desk. Cathy rolled her chair back a few feet to escape the fumes. I stood up.

"Leroy...you know we won't give you money."

"Awww. Come on." He looked around. "Where's your fearless leader?"

"Playing tennis, I guess," I answered.

"Yeah. With his little wifey who rode her bikey over."

"I think not, Leroy." I walked around the desk and gestured to go into the book room. "Olive works at Mariposa Gallery," I said.

"Jesus, Mary and Joseph! Don't give Leroy a hearty attack!"

"And I think I saw a sharp-toothed young woman named Holly assisting Olive."

"Figures Olive took up with those punks."

"I thought she only liked dolls."

"I'm thirsty."

"There's a water fountain in the foyer."

"Aww…You're a hard one, little missy!" Leroy squinted at me and tilted his head.

"If you must know, and it's actually none of your business, I am very fragile right now. Don't rag at me. Why aren't you surprised that Olive works with those girls?"

"Because she hated Charlie. She probably hired those girls to bring false charges against him."

"Why? What did Charlie ever do to Olive?"

"He married her."

"Jesus, Mary and Joseph!"

Leroy crossed himself. "Amen, sister! Now how about you joining me somewhere for a little something? You can tell Old Leroy why you feel so fragile."

I started to laugh in spite of myself. I put my hands on his greasy sleeve. I shook my head as tears filled my eyes. I was so touched that he seemed to care. A little warmth. A little something.

Twenty Six

Two-dozen tea roses were on the dining room table in a huge, gaudy crystal vase. My first thought was that was his mother's vase. My second thought was that the house smelled like a funeral parlor. I opened some windows. I let Suki in. Stop being such a bitch, I told myself. John knew that tea roses were my mother's and my favorite flower. He planted a tea rose in the back yard after she was killed in an auto accident. He was trying now. And I was not.

This was my last week working part-time. I wanted to enjoy my afternoon while I could. But the smell of roses kept reminding me of my troubled marriage. And the passive way I have led my life. So far.

After a soothing BLT, 100 Doritos and a Diet Coke I curled up in bed with Suki, an afghan, and *A Cinnamon Summer*. I had to be in total denial for a few hours. I just could not think about making decisions anymore. Not to mention what to make of the tangled, incestuous couplings in the art world. (Note to let my Inspector know!) I was worn out mentally, physically, and emotionally. Whenever I needed a vacation from reality, I turned to books. Well, time to see what's was going on with Chance and Lily. I probably should be Googling divorce lawyers.

I read:

Lily stepped into a claw foot tub filled with bubbly, lavender scented, steamy water. Ouch! She turned off the hot water to let the cold run a while. She dipped one dolphin decaled toe through the thick suds and swirled the cool water to the back of the tub. Perfect! Ah, she said and she lowered herself into the bath. What relief after the long drive and rude interruptions! She lit her Aveda Rosemary Mint Travel Candle.

(I used those! Tina checked out my bathroom!)

She thought about the pleasant, light dinner she had shared with her aunt earlier that evening. Lily had changed into an embroidered shift from Mexico. Aunt Geneva wore denim overalls. She served cold chicken, quinoa and kale salad. Lily passed on the offered tumbler of scotch. She sipped white pinot grigio that came from a lint covered bottle her aunt found in the laundry room. I have to find a liquor store, Lily thought. They spoke briefly about her father. Aunt Geneva expressed sincere grief over the loss of her estranged brother, and did not ask any questions about Lily's marriage to Brad. The only outward affection from her aunt was a hand on the shoulder or a pat on the back. Didn't exactly make Lily break down and cry.

(She'd probably done enough already, poor little thing.)

Her aunt's house was filled with strange but charming objects de arte: woven basketballs, acrylic cubes of newly minted coins, various Limoges figurines...Illustrated pages from children's books hung on the walls. Her home smelled fresh and clean with a faint underlying note of Chanel #5 perfume. Thank goodness because Geneva smoked like a chimney when they sat outside on the porch after dinner. Lily snapped off ¼ of a dark chocolate Kit Kat. Lily always liked a little something sweet after dinner. But she never ate the whole thing!

(Of course not.)

"Thank you for letting me come here, Aunt Geneva," Lily said.

"Oh you're welcome. You were always welcome here, but I guess you never knew that."

Lily did not want to discuss her family's lack of communication. She changed the subject.

"So, who is this Chance Nail?"

"Oh! Him! I was waiting for you to ask!" Aunt *Geneva started laughing, then had a coughing fit. She stubbed out her butt in a flower pot. "Quite a specimen, huh? If I were 50 years younger...watch out!"* She lit *another Virginia Slim.*

"He's very abrupt!" Lily said and snapped off another *¼ of Kit Kat in spite of her good intentions.*

"Chance was raised in a series of foster homes. Tragic past with his parents. Don't know all the details. But Edgar adopted him as a pre-teen. He was pretty feral. Still is in a way..."

"Who's Edgar?"

"Don't pretend you have never heard of Edgar!"

Lily stood up. "Honest, Aunt Geneva! I never!"

"You never heard that I was having an affair with a married man for almost 40 years?"

(How did she get away with that?)

"I heard about the affair. I never knew his name. When can I meet him?" Lily sat back down. She didn't mention how her parents thought Geneva was living a scandalous life--having an affair with a married man.

"Oh he died three years ago. His wife is still in a mental hospital where she's been since her twenties. After Chance got out of prison he moved here. I'm his family."

(Oh that's how! Wifey was away. Far, far away.)

Lily stuffed the rest of the Kit Kat in her mouth. "Prison? What for?"

"Something stupid. But on appeal his actions were found justified. He was exonerated...but Chance has issues."

(Oh...a sex maniac ready to explode?)

Reclining now in her bath, Lily trickled water down from her fingers onto her breasts. Her small, pink nipples hardened. Felt so good. Stop! What was she doing? Oh yeah...thinking about Chance's issues. She needed to get out of the tub, out of fantasyland, and into bed. With her dog. She heard whining. Tulip must need to go out. Lily dried her rosy, warm, fragrant skin. She wrapped a fluffy towel around her and stepped out of the bathroom. Right into Chance Nail.

(As it should be.)

"What are you doing here?" Lily screamed and pulled the towel more tightly around her.

"What are you doing here?" Chance shouted.

"I live here!"

"I told you the cottage was not ready!" He wore cut-offs, a hoodie, and flip flops. He carried a tool box. A very large keychain hung down from his belt. His aqua eyes bored right into her. Again.

Lily stood on her tiptoes and yelled: "Get out! Now!"

Bruno came galloping around the corner, jumped up on Lily knocking her down. Tulip ran behind but sat down suddenly to watch the excitement. Bruno bit the bottom of Lily's towel and pulled it off her. She tried to yank it back, but his jaws were too strong. Bruno, Tulip, and the towel disappeared.

(Good dog!)

Lily looked up at Chance and froze. He locked his eyes on hers. She could not run for a cover. She could not look away. She could not move under his laser gaze. Finally, after what seemed like an hour instead of a minute, Chance slowly put down his tools. He bent over, took Lily's hands and pulled her up.

"Are you all right?" he asked.

"Yes," she said breathlessly.

Not breaking eye contact, he unzipped his hoodie and slipped it off. His long blonde hair fell loose and wild. His bare chest was lean and tan with a few manly hairs. She started to shiver. Not with cold. Something different was affecting her entire body. It was like the chills one had while running a fever. Chance gently draped his sweatshirt around her shoulders. Then he reached down *to zip it up. His hands lightly brushed over the silky blonde curls between her legs as he inserted the slider into the bottom stop. His long fingers pulled the zipper up very carefully: over the curvaceous hips, the rounded tummy, the tiny waist, and all the while he drank in her body with those devilish eyes. Before the zipper passed her breasts, his eyes became hooded, and he stopped. He looked at her through his long lashes.*

(Tina! How can anyone see through one's eyelashes?)

"Oh!" Lily sighed. Expecting the worst.

(She hoped!)

Chance grabbed her around the waist and crushed her to his body. He smelled of sand and sea. She felt the sun's warmth on her breasts as they pressed into his bronzed chest.

"I'm not done in here," he snarled.

Well! I certainly forgot everything in my life for a few minutes. Thank you, Tina! I will practice delayed gratification and continue later. I heaved the manuscript under the bed. Now I have to think about dinner. Probably meat loaf. The boys will groan. I needed some comfort food. They can pour red chili on it. Oh why do I worry about such things? While my home life was going down the toilet? I closed my eyes. I imagined James zipping a hoodie up my nude body.

I awoke from a mind-deadening nap to Max and Douglas exclaiming over whether to eat ribs or links. I walked into the kitchen.

"Dad brought home Rudy's Barbeque, Mom!" Max said.

"Oh happy day!" I chirped. John was opening up a bottle of wine.

"I am so hungry!" Douglas said as he took plates down from the cabinet. Max brought silverware and napkins. He opened the cartons of potato salad and coleslaw. He stuck serving spoons in each. Douglas poured glasses of milk. What a burst of activity! So all it took was barbeque?

John held up two glasses of white wine. "Let's go outside."

"Don't smoke on the deck!" Douglas called after us. "I can smell it through the kitchen window!"

I followed John outside. He set our wines on a stool. He took my hands.

"I'm sorry. I was wrong." He hugged me gently. He lightly kissed my lips.

I quietly stared into his sad eyes for a long time. I felt nothing. I turned to look through the kitchen window. Douglas and Max were watching us. I felt everything.

Twenty Seven

I parked my car as usual on the east side of the ghetto Walgreen's and started walking to the Fine Arts Center. Such a colorful stretch of Central Avenue with the combinations of students walking to the university, beggars on every corner, motley crowds at the bus stops, and university employees like myself. I trudged along wondering what to do about my marriage. We tried couple's counseling a few years ago. I sat there and cried in a tee, jeans and flip-flops. John sat there tight-lipped in a suit and tie. The therapist said that we both went from A to C. We have conflict in our marriage (A), and we jump automatically to catastrophe (C). "Try going to B," he said. "Go home and practice discussing a difference of opinion. Like, I don't know…what color sofa to buy." I cried even more.

"They say" going to marriage counseling is the kiss of death for a married couple. All it did for me was to strengthen my resolve to throw myself into activities that drove me quite crazy so I couldn't think about my marriage anymore. Now I was. I did not like the way I felt and didn't want to spend God knows how many years feeling this way. But I will maintain. I thought about the Graduate Exhibition opening gala tonight. What will I wear? Who cared?

I walked way around four staggering, dirty, shabbily dressed men moving in a line across the sidewalk blocking my way. They were laughing and shouting in another language. I passed through a cloud of alcoholic fumes. 8:45 AM. Party Hardy! Earlier the better. "Good morning!" they shouted at me.

A woman popped up between two parked cars. "Sister! Sister! Please help me! I have a trach," she rasped holding her hand over her throat. She held her other hand open in a beseeching pose. I had liked her act before. I let her finish her spiel. "I need bus money to get to the hospital to have it removed! It's infected! Have mercy, sister!"

"I gave you money last week!" I said. She dropped her hand from her very normal neck. No incision. No breathing tube.

"Well, God bless you anyway!" She said in a normal voice. I watched her cover her throat again and approach another person.

I resumed walking ahead. A bicyclist riding on the sidewalk was coming straight at me. She whizzed past me so fast that I felt the rider's long scarf brush my arm as I hopped off the sidewalk into the gutter. The woman's hair was in a French Roll. A doll's head peeked out a rear wicker basket. Olive! Rude! No bell! No horn! Was she trying to run me down? I was getting paranoid.

I decided to turn off Central and walk down the street a block away. Silver Avenue was a quiet older neighborhood shaded by tall trees. I loved running my fingers along the well-kept shrubbery along the sidewalk. Smelled so fresh. Calmed me down. After several blocks, I walked back to Central to cross onto the university campus. I could smell the delicious aroma coming from Einstein's Bagels. What I wouldn't give for an Everything Bagel slathered with cream cheese. But I read in *Prevention Magazine* that one bagel had as many calories as five pieces of white bread. I will control myself.

I watched someone dumpster diving behind Einstein's. Was that Leroy? I called out "Leroy?" He rose up with a bagel in his mouth and two in his hand. He turned around, saw me, and took the bagel out of his mouth.

"Good morning, young lady!"

"Having brekky?"

"They throw away all the day old bagels. They're still good. Want one?"

"No thanks."

"I'm thirsty!"

"What else is new? I'll buy you some coffee." I called the Art Museum. Cathy was already there. I told her I was going to be late.

Leroy plopped himself down at one of bistro tables in front of the shop. I went inside to order two coffees. "I could use some schmear!" he yelled.

"Sad," I shouted.

"You are a Missy Thing!" Leroy roared with laughter.

I brought out the coffees and sat down. "Beautiful day to be alive!" Leroy said as he soaked part of his bagel in coffee until it softened. Then gummed it happily. I did not smell alcohol on him…just some faint garbage fumes.

"So true…," I said.

"Why don't you tell me why you feel fragile?"

I did not want to talk about myself. I could start crying and ruin my make-up. I racked my feeble brain to change the subject.

"Do you know why Charlie was in the Fine Arts Center the night he was killed?"

"Well, he took showers there."

"What?"

"Oh yeah…he showered in the Theatre and Dance men's dressing room in the basement. And had a locker. I go to St. Martin's. They have food."

"How did he get in?"

"The Fine Arts Library stays open until ten at night. The doors to the Fine Arts Center are only locked after they close. Didn't they tell you that when you were hired? It's a security issue! People! Honestly!" Leroy lisped.

I pressed on with my own agenda: "Has anyone looked in his locker?"

"I don't know."

"Do you know his locker number?"

"No."

"Well! Do the police know this?"

"I don't know." Leroy reached across the table and took my hand. His fingers were calloused, dirty and rough, but warm. I felt ashamed that I wanted to wash my hands immediately. "Enough about the dead. I know you need to talk. Here I am. All ears."

"Thank you, but I have to get to work." And call my Inspector.

"Don't take so much to heart…whatever is bothering you."

I got up. "I'll be fine. See you!"

Leroy smiled. "See you later, alligator."

"After awhile, crocodile," I said as I walked away.

Leroy laughed until he choked. I started to turn back out of concern. Leroy held up a flask, waved me away, and took a big swig.

Twenty Eight

Linda was waiting for me when I walked into the museum.

"You're late," she said.

"I called Cathy. Where is she?"

"Bathroom. So I had to come down here."

"Thank you," I said and walked around her to the closet in the bookroom to put away my purse. I felt her eyes boring holes in my back.

She was still staring at me as I sat down behind the front desk and said: "You can go now. Thank you again for your support."

"Right." Linda looked up and down around the shop. She lifted a handful of *milagros* out of a bowl and dropped them back in one by one. Plink. Plink. Plink. "You gonna sell a lot of stuff tonight?"

"Of course."

"You better."

"Museum administrators need travel money? Conferences in Hawaii coming up?" I asked innocently.

Linda glared at me and walked out. She ignored Cathy who came back in at the same time.

"She is not a team player!" Cathy exclaimed as we watched Linda turn and stomp down the hallway.

"I'll say. Don't pay attention! Let's get the shop ready."

Cathy and I dusted, rearranged books, tee shirts, journals and pottery. We windexed the jewelry display cases. I made sure the art cards and postcards were in their right slots. I had stocked the Museum Shop with a lot of merchandise. I enjoyed making the space colorful and inviting. But it was a lot more work for all of us in the shop. And we did not get to keep the money we earned every month. The museum administration used our healthy profits to fly to conferences. I felt like we were banging our heads against the wall trying to make this shop a success. No wonder Pat only sold a few art magnets.

We greeted visitors who seemed to be excited by the Graduate Exhibition. They chattered among themselves. That is a good omen for the success of a show. Three women stood in front of the wall hung with used tea bags. They stared. Then started discussing. I could hear every word since the exhibit was at the bottom of the stairs below the front desk.

"Well, I don't know what to think," one said.

"I want to know what the red pins mean," another said.

A lady pointed. "Look. The white thumb tacks are up there, but the artist put a few down here. The reds are scattered, and they have a different shape! Push pins not thumb tacks!"

"True. No pattern?"

"Not that I can see now. Let's follow the line of red."

They stared. They traced the line of red pins in the air.

"Could it spell something?

"Not in English."

"Is it an outline of a form?"

"I can't tell!"

"Must mean something."

"It's a mystery. Let's come back tonight and meet the artist."

"Great idea! I am intrigued."

Cathy and I looked at each other. Our hands flew up to cover our mouths. We could not laugh! To think we gave the artist the red push pins to finish hanging her tea bags. Ah…collaboration…art.

We closed early to set up the main gallery for the opening. The caterers from the Student Union Building were rolling in banquet tables through the rear door of the main gallery. We let the drummer in from the Jazz Band to put up his trap set. A man was connecting electrical wiring. I decided to visit the Theatre and Dance office before I went home. I had a few questions…before I called James.

Twenty Nine

The Theatre and Dance office was just around the corner from the Art Museum. I entered the small, windowless room. It was crowded with two desks, a chair, a wall of crooked mail slots with curling nametags, a door leading to a smaller copy room, and another closed door with CHAIR printed on it. A man sat at a desk working on a computer. He didn't look up. I moved closer to his desk. He didn't look up. I moved closer. He didn't look up.

"Excuse me," I said politely.

The man continued typing for a while. Stopped and turned slowly to face me. He was young, handsome, dark hair perfectly combed with a razor sharp part, crisply dressed, and smelled good. He stood out in this shabby office. He did not smile.

"Yes?" he said.

"Hello!" I said. "My name is Caro, and I work at the Art Museum. I--"

"I know."

"Well! Fine Arts news gets around. I'll say."

Silence. He looked at me with hooded eyes.

I forged on. "I wanted to ask you some questions about the men's dressing room in the basement."

"What do you want to know?"

"Perhaps you heard that a man was found dead in--"

"I know."

"OK. You know. Someone told me that he used the Theatre dressing room shower, and that he may have had a locker here. I don't know which one, but is there any way one can look in the lockers. There may be evidence--"

"A lot of homeless people use our showers and lockers. It's disgusting. But I am not about to snap the locks off all the lockers now. I only do that at the end of spring semester. Come back with a court order." He swiveled back to his computer.

"I will. Thanks, uh…"

"Clarence."

"Thank you, Clarence. Ever so."

My Inspector will meet with the College of Fine Arts Dean. We will not deal with that bitch.

Thirty

I needed to relax before going back for the graduate reception. I was having carry out for everyone tonight, so I didn't have to worry about dinner. I ripped off my torture bra, jewelry and work clothes. I changed into plaid cotton pajama pants and a Target tissue tee. Ahhh. Relief. I made a sandwich with the usual mountain of chips, popped open a Diet Coke, and balanced it on the table next to my bed. I hauled *A Cinnamon Summer* out from under the bed. Suki jumped up and flopped on John's pillow. Where did I leave off? Oh yeah... Chance wasn't finished in there. Ha! I read:

Chance abruptly pushed her away. He touched her breasts lightly as he finished zipping up the hoodie. Then he yanked opened the front door and slammed it closed. Lily broke out in goose bumps. Her legs went weak. She thought she might faint. She stood frozen in place. She couldn't move. Then the door burst open. Chance walked in carrying her precious boxer. He gently put her down. Tulip jumped up on Chance again and again.

(Smart dog!)

"Stay here with your mommy, little girl," he said. Chance gave Lily a piercing glance and left. Tulip also gave Lily a look as she plopped down on the floor.

Well, dang, Lily thought. She took off the hoodie. She pressed her face into it as she stumbled into the bedroom and collapsed on the bed. She breathed in Chance's manly, musky scent before placing it on her pillow. Tulip jumped on the bed and curled up on the sweatshirt. "Now that's too much!" Lily laughed. She rubbed Tulip's ears. Then she got up, put on her white eyelet nightgown, slathered herself in lavender lotion and crawled back into bed. She managed to pull one sleeve of the hoodie out from under Tulip. She curled up with it in her hand.

But, alas, sleep did not come. Lily tossed and turned. She was hot. She imagined what could have happened between her and Chance. How would it feel to make love to someone else? Would she know how to do anything right? Brad told her once that she was mechanical in bed. Lily cried all night. But what else could she do when he was working her body like she was a machine in a gym? She went limp. Brad was the mechanical and sloppy one in bed she realized. She will not own that insult any longer!

(You go, girl!)

Lily got very hot. And hungry. She sat up. What's in the cupboards?

(Hopefully a large bottle of vodka, spray cheese and crackers. A few ciggies.)

Lily slipped her feet into a pair of powder blue feathered leather mules and went into the kitchen. Hmmm. All the staples were there: flour, sugar, spices, seasonings, milk, coffee, eggs, butter, cheeses, tomatoes, kale. A bowl of fresh fruit. A baguette. Thank you, Aunt Geneva! She found a blue gingham apron in a drawer and tied it around her waist. She pulled a big bowl out of the lower cabinet and started throwing in a little of this and a little of that. She grated two apples. She sprinkled them with cinnamon sugar. She added them to the bowl. Then she sat down with the bowl between her thighs and beat everything 300 times with a wooden spoon. No electric beaters for her! Oh she felt a lot better! Then she poured the mixture into a greased baking pan. The apple cake was done in 30 minutes. The cottage smelled so warm and good. Lily put a leash on Tulip, and they sat on the front porch while the cake cooled. She looked at the sky. She saw a shooting star. She wished…she wished…she wished for true love. Was it too late for her? She shook her head. She wiped a tear from her eye. Then she treated herself to a small corner of cake. So delicious. So comforting. She cleaned up the kitchen. She washed all the dishes by hand. The warm soapy water soothed her. Lily slept soundly hugging Chance's hoodie.

(Dreaming of Chance finishing up, I'm sure.)

"Why this was fabulous!" exclaimed Aunt Geneva. She licked her fingers to pick up the remaining crumbs of apple cake left on the plate..

Lily smiled. She and her aunt were having coffee and cake out on her aunt's porch the next morning. Geneva was still in her overalls. Lily had on a white dotted swiss short-sleeved blouse and madras shorts. Aquamarine studs shone in her ears. A silver bracelet with little bells tinkled on her wrist. A black velvet headband held the riotous curls away from her face. She only applied a few swipes of mascara and a bit of lipstick. This wasn't Texas, after all! Her skin had a natural glow for some reason.

"You just threw this together late last night?" Geneva asked.

"Yes. Thank you for stocking the cottage so generously!"

"Let me know if you need anything else."

"Well, Chance mentioned to me that he had more work to do on the cottage..."

"Oh! He's a perfectionist!"

"Is he?"

"He does things right, I tell you."

(I'm certainly looking forward to reading about all his perfect moves).

"You think?"

"Chance wants to run an extra electrical wire somewhere. I don't know. Electricity. Power. Something. He already talked to me about it."

"Really? I'm going to stay away from the cottage until he's finished. He got agitated last night when I was there."

(He wasn't the only one.)

"Maybe there was an exposed wire somewhere? He didn't want you to get shocked...

(Ha! Too late!)

Say, why don't you take some of this marvelous apple cake over to Flo's Ice Cream Shoppe? She used to sell bakery products. She might start up again. She brews *good coffee, too. Go on…meet Flo! Leave Chance to do his thing."*

"Can Tulip stay in your house? I don't want her around the cottage bothering Chance."

"Of course you may leave her here."

Lily took Chance's hoodie out of her African bag. She tossed it on the table. Tulip sniffed it and wagged her tail.

"Please give this to Chance when you see him," Lily said.

"He must have gotten too hot working last night."

"I guess."

Geneva smelled the hoodie. "Lavender," she whispered. She looked at Lily with raised eyebrows.

I put the manuscript back under the bed. Thank you, Tina! But I am looking forward to more heat! I closed my eyes and thought about my Inspector. And all the work he had to finish up. And how much I could help him finish up. We could finish up together. At the same time. Now there's a happy thought, indeed. I drifted into a twilight sleep.

Thirty One

I parked near the Frontier Restaurant. The city did not ticket at night. I hoped. The Fine Arts Center was just across Central Avenue past the Bookstore. I did not want to walk too far in my black La Duca Italian t-strap heels. They looked very good with the Gap wrap dress in jewel tones that I was wearing. I felt happy to dress up. This day had so many emotional ups and downs. I was determined to enjoy the remains of the day. I left John and the boys eating pizza. They told me to have a good time. I will if it kills me. I felt very exited that I had so much information for James. I will call him tomorrow. I must focus on gaiety and art.

I waited at the corner for the light to change. I looked through the glass windows of the Frontier, an Albuquerque institution for decades. The sixties were alive and well in this town! Hippy dippy long-haired people of all ages hung out there. Coaches took their teams there after games. People going to events at Popejoy Hall, all dressed up in their formal best, ate there. Study groups met there. Hamburgers, breakfast burritos, pancakes, huge homemade cinnamon rolls, red and green chili, chopped steak, southwestern fries--all consistently delicious no matter what time of day or night. My son Peter insisted on stopping at the Frontier when he got off the plane from Austin and again on the way back to Austin, with a dozen of their fluffy flour tortillas in his backpack. I was getting hungry.

The light changed. I crossed the street, walked past the bookstore and architecture building into the Fine Arts Center.

I heard music as I walked through the foyer. The museum was lit up. The doors wide open. No crypt look tonight! All three work studies were there. Cathy, Mike and Alana were dressed up and looked so attractive. Pat stood close by dressed so prettily in a blue shift. I was so thankful to work with them. Such a wonderful support group.

In the middle of the main gallery the banquet tables were set up groaning with food: shrimp, short skewers of Asian chicken, guacamole, cheeses, baguettes, bite-sized crab quiches, crudités, fresh fruit platters, and, I was relieved to see, a lot of tortilla chips. A bartender stood behind a table in the southwest corner pouring wine. The Jazz Band played in the opposite corner. What a sound! Some couples were dancing in any available open floor space. The Art Museum administrators circulated among the *hoi polloi*; still in black, every unmovable bob do in place. How special to see them actually in the museum. No Linda. Too bad. Ken was not there, either. He was probably home drinking a large glass of vodka. I could hear Roland's booming voice above the band as he worked the crowd like a circus barker. The featured artists chatted animatedly about their art with the visitors. They were dressed in their best boho style. The three ladies who were puzzled by the tea bags earlier in the day surrounded the artist. Wished I knew how she explained the meaning of the red push pins!

I told the students to get a plate of food while I manned the front desk. Shoppers jammed the area. I started to sell a lot of merchandise. Pat helped me. We laughed as we collected money, ran charge cards, and bagged items. We danced together to the music in between customers. Cathy joined us. I was having fun. Then I saw my Inspector walk in with a woman.

James was wearing khaki chinos, a blue gingham shirt, and an aquamarine tie. His thick, wavy dark auburn hair looked like he had just run his fingers through it. I wanted to run over and run my fingers through it. But I didn't. James and the woman stood just inside the museum talking. My legs went weak. I sat down in the chair behind the desk

Pat nudged me. "Caro! Look! That handsome policeman is here. Didn't you say you knew him?"

"Yes," I whispered.

"He looks like that guy who used to be on *Fringe,*" Pat said.

"Yes! And he now is in *The Affair*. Do you watch *The Affair*, Caro?" Cathy said.

"Yes," I whispered.

"He's married to the gal who is having the affair!" Pat said.

"I can't believe she's cheating on him! Can you, Caro?" Cathy asked.

"No," I whispered.

I watched Roland bound up the stairs two at a time to greet James and his companion. He led them to the bar.

"Caro…your turn to get some food," I heard Cathy say. I got up and walked out of the museum. "Where are you going?" she asked.

"I need some fresh air." Outside I took several deep breaths. I gazed at the stars. I went back in.

The front desk crew looked concerned. I gave them a big smile. Pat handed me a glass of wine over the counter. At the banquet table I picked up a plate and started tossing God knows what food on it. I started back to the front desk.

"Mrs. Steele." James blocked my path before I reached the stairs.

"Oh hi!" I gushed.

"What a wonderful opening. May I introduce Lt. Jane Keyes from the Campus Police."

I balanced the wine on my plate and shook hands with Jane. She had short blonde hair, wore black slacks, black boots, and a purple silk blouse. She was in her forties, I guessed, fresh faced and slender. She was almost as tall as James--an inch or two shorter. She must be six feet tall I calculated quickly while smiling sincerely, I hoped.

"Welcome to the Art Museum," I said.

"I'm so glad Roland invited us," Jane said.

"He's quite the guy."

"I know that artist over there!" Jane exclaimed suddenly. "She's my neighbor. Excuse me." She left us alone.

"What a great band," James said. "May I have this dance?" Before I could answer, he took my plate and set it on a table. He put one arm around my waist. I put one hand in his and one on his shoulder.

I looked into his sea green eyes. I was lost. I was going to Hell. I did not care.

"You dance like you swim," he said. "Easy."

"Do I now," I said.

We danced. He was easy, too.

"Jane and I are working together on Charles's murder."

"I have been working on Charles's murder also."

James spun me around and pulled me back tightly against him. And kept me there. Our bodies pressed tightly together as we swayed to the music.

"Doing my job for me again, Mrs. Steele?"

"Every chance I get."

"Will you please show me the handicapped lift?"

"Again?"

"My memory is so bad lately."

"I'm sorry."

I left his embrace to get my keys.

***

The lower gallery was empty. I unlocked the door to the lift closet. We entered. James shut the door behind us. I threw my arms around him. I kissed him passionately.

He kissed me back. Passionately. "What do you know, Mrs. Steele?" he finally asked.

We were nose to nose. "Charles showered here."

"Where?" James tilted his head and kissed me lightly. "This is…" he kissed me. "A big…" He kissed me. "Place." He kissed me.

"Theatre…basement…," I sighed. I kissed him gently.

"What else?" He drew me even closer. I clung to him.

James stopped my answer with a gentle kiss. He just touched the tip of his tongue to mine. I didn't move. For a long time. Then I drew back. We looked at each other. I softly put my lips on his. I inhaled his breath. "He had a locker," I whispered.

My legs went weak. I leaned back against the wall. My shoulder hit a switch. The lift started to rise. James whirled around. He flattened himself against the wall next to me. We watched the lift go higher in front of us. It screeched to a stop at the ground floor hallway door. We started laughing so hard that we slid down and sat in hysterics. We had a delightful view of what lay under the handicapped lift: rusty springs, dead roaches, dirt, stained linoleum, nails, rocks, and something sparkly. And red. We sobered up quickly. James crawled over to get the object and showed it to me. I blew on it as he held it in front of my face.

"Looks like a ruby," I said. "Did I ever tell you about Olive?"

Thirty Two

We sat side by side in a window booth after we'd stood in line to order a luscious Napoleon, a chicken salad sandwich, and coffee. I was very hungry.

After leaving the museum in the good care of my work-studies, James and I drove to the Flying Star Café in Nob Hill to talk. The Frontier was too noisy. He followed me in his car.

"Let me sit on your left," James had said.

"Why?"

"I'm left handed. Our arms won't get in the way…of each other."

"Happy thought, indeed." I cut the sandwich in half for us. We devoured it. I picked up my fork to start on the Napoleon but started waving it around in the air. "I want to tell you more about the shower and locker."

James dropped his fork. He gently lowered mine to the table. "Please do, Mrs. Steele."

"Leroy told me that Charles took showers in the Theatre Department's men's dressing rooms in the Fine Arts Center basement at night. He had a locker there, too. The Theatre Department prissy administrative assistant told me that we needed a court order to open a locker."

"I'll take care of it. No court order needed."

"When?"

"Soon." James gave me my fork. "Shall we?"

I put the fork down. "Seems to me that this investigation is going slowly. So far I have gotten a lot of crucial information for this case. What have you been doing? Is it because he was homeless? He was a talented man! Brought down by forces beyond his control. And beaten to death!"

"Charlie's homeless state has nothing to do with how slow this investigation is going, Mrs. Steele. This is complicated. I have accessed Roland's bank records. He has deposited thousands of dollars into an account every month for the last year. This is over his salary. Money is coming from an unknown source. Then some of that money is withdrawn on a regular basis. We don't know where it went."

"Building on an extension to his house for dolls," I said.

"What?"

"Oh nothing...Roland comes from a wealthy family. Maybe he's drawing on a trust fund."

"Not from his trust fund. We checked. The mystery funds are deposited in an account with an interesting name: Alianza Abiquiu."

"Georgia O'Keeffe lived in Abiquiu, New Mexico."

"Where is that?"

"Northern New Mexico. A beautiful place."

"I'd like to visit sometime," James said.

"Oh would you now?"

We looked at each other a long time.

James finally handed me my fork. "We just hired a forensic accountant," he continued. "Charles closed out a very large bank account a few months after he left the university."

"To build his cabin up in El Morro?"

"It must have been a very fancy one," James said. "And it burned down a year ago. Suspected arson. His art studio destroyed. And all his money was in there. No insurance."

"Oh that's awful!"

"When I interviewed the poker players, they said that Roland got food poisoning from lunch, left the game early and retired to his room. He was sick the rest of that day and night. He did join them for breakfast the next morning before they all got on the train back to Albuquerque. I am checking into flights between Kansas City and Albuquerque to see if Roland could have been here the night Charles was killed and made it back to Kansas City by morning. I have been investigating, Mrs. Steele."

I looked at him a long time. "Is this you talking like a policeman?"

James stared at me.

I leaned over and whispered in his ear. "I really like it."

"There's more where that came from, Mrs. Steele."

"Really now?" I had a hot flash.

We shared the Napoleon. We watched each other as we chewed the thinly iced puff pastry layered with creamy yellow filling. Flakes of crust flew from our mouths. Who cared? We drank our coffee. James stretched out his legs under the table to put his feet up on the seat in front of us. I draped my legs over his. My dress hiked up to mid thigh. I slowly licked my fork. I felt so satisfied. Like a big cat. I was not myself.

"So are you going to tell me about Olive?" James said.

"Oh her! Leroy told me that she used to be married to Charles! The College of Fine Arts is an incestuous hot bed of intrigue!"

"The best kind of place, I've found," James said, laughing.

"Never a dull moment, I'm sure...but I am almost certain that one of the girls who accused Charles of harassment works for her. I think that is too much of a coincidence."

"Albuquerque is a big city but a small town, Mrs. Steele."

"Hmmm. I sound like a conspiracy theorist, but they may have worked together to plot Charles's downfall and who knows what else! And who knows why?"

James took my hand in his. He turned it over and kissed my palm. I was saving my best information for a final powerful delivery, but I could not speak for a moment.

"Are you listening to me?" I finally asked.

"I always listen to you, Mrs. Steele," James said. He kissed my palm again.

"Olive wears a skull ring with ruby eyes," I said weakly in spite of my dramatic intentions.

Suddenly his feet hit the floor. My legs collapsed. James dropped my hand to take out his notebook. "Please repeat everything you know about Olive," he said.

"Let's go down the block, Inspector Hutchinson." I rearranged my wrap dress. "You can meet her yourself."

***

Mariposa Gallery was an explosion of light, color and consumers. I could tell that James was impressed with the art. He left my side to walk around reading labels. I looked for Olive. There she was. Dressed in an electric blue silky jump suit, black patent leather jeweled Grecian sandals, and a statement necklace of large turquoise and silver flowers. Platinum hair done in an elaborate French roll. Huge silver hoops in her ears. She must have sensed me staring at her. She slithered over.

"Why aren't you at the Art Museum?" she asked while looking me up and down. I felt like Suzy housewife in my Gap dress.

"Why hello, Olive. The reception is over by now."

"Don't you need to clean up?"

"Haha," I said without smiling. "The caterers are in charge of that. And my student employees are locking up."

"You must trust those young people. Does Roland know you've given them such responsibility?"

"Of course he does. They are trustworthy. They wouldn't have keys otherwise. Roland is very particular about who gets keys to the Art Museum. Don't you think?"

"I wouldn't know. But I am often amazed at the caliber of people he hires to work at the museum. I have often warned him to be more discriminating..."

"Have you now..." I interrupted and felt a hand on my elbow. James.

Olive plastered a wide smile on her face. Her veneers flashed a blinding white. "Hello! My name is Olive. Welcome to Mariposa Gallery." She stuck out her Vamp nail polished veiny hand. James took it in his. His eyes flickered briefly at the skull ring. He smiled his devastating smile. "Are you with her?" Olive jerked her head in my direction never taking her eyes off him.

"Yes. Mrs. Steele has recommended your gallery highly. I am new to town and always looking for beautiful objects of art."

"Well, you have come to the right place, Mr...?"

"Hutchinson. Inspector James Hutchinson."

Olive quickly withdrew her hand. She blinked several times, shot a glance at me, but turned gaily back to James.

"What are you interested in, James?' Olive asked.

"Anything colorful. Helps my mood."

"I could tell right away you loved color. Not many men could carry off an aquamarine tie. May I fix you up a little? Seems like you have had some activity lately." Olive reached up to tighten the knot in James's tie. Then she curled her fingers under the knot and slowly slid her hand down the length of the tie. Olive held the tip of the tie in her left hand while she reached up and swiftly ran her hand down the tie again. She let go. "There. All better now."

"Thank you, Olive," James said with a bemused smile.

Jesus, I thought. Shameless woman!

"Please let me know if I can help you with anything, James."

"Oh I certainly will. You can count on it, Olive."

James started wandering around. Olive's face resumed a hatchet profile for a few seconds when she shot me a glance. I was seething. I bent over the jewelry cases to hide the emotional reaction probably written all over my face. I walked from one display to the next. I got tired of looking at all the overpriced bling. I had to get out of there. I walked toward to door to wait outside for James. I passed the cash register where a young girl dressed in black with purple hair sat on a stool. Next to her on another stool sat a ballerina doll. She was so beautiful: turquoise tutu, a lavender leotard with tiny pink roses encased in lace at the neck, dark blue eyes, long lashes, red hair piled on top of her head surrounded by more tiny roses, mesh pink tights, and satin toe shoes. I used to love my dolls. But I played with them. This one must have escaped from the addition.

"Have a nice evening!" the girl said with a sharp toothed smile.

I leaned against a light pole. I needed a cigarette. But did not want to smell (or taste!) like an ashtray. I watched the traffic going up and down Central. I looked at all the people walking around Nob Hill. I watched the Scot's Dog Groomer's blue neon Scottie flash on and off. I took deep Yoga breaths.

"Why did you bring that inspector to the gallery?" I turned around. There was Olive in full attack mode. Her mascara was dripping. A few platinum hairs hung free from her French Roll. "Does Roland know that you are hanging out with the police?"

"It's none of Roland's business who I socialize with," I said.

"I think it is his business. And you're not minding your own business. Just stick to your little shop job and stay out of what doesn't concern you."

"I don't know what you're talking about, Olive. What ever do you mean?"

"You know what I mean. Don't play stupid with me. I read you like a book."

"That's a cliché, Olive."

"I don't give a shit. I'm going to tell Roland about you."

"What about me? That I brought you some possible business? That I was with a person who I knew a year ago? Oh yes. It was another murder case. I helped him solve it, actually. We have been talking about poor dead Charles. I believe you knew him. Very well, I understand. And talk about trustworthy student help...you have one. Or two. But they're not students anymore, are they? I guess they graduated early, if at all..."

"You know nothing. Don't make trouble for me. I'm warning you…"

"Ready to go, Mrs. Steele?" James appeared at my side. "Good night, Olive. I will return. You have a wonderful gallery."

"Good-night, James." Huge smile. "I was just telling Caro how much I looked forward to seeing you again."

I coughed.

"I look forward to seeing you, too."

Olive gave me one last poisonous look. She went inside.

I kept up with James's quick strides down the sidewalk. "How much of that did you hear?" I asked.

"Enough. Olive doesn't have a clue how much I look forward to seeing her."

"She'll jack off your tie again."

"Language, Mrs. Steele."

"And I forgot to tell you that she tried to run me down on the sidewalk this morning on her bike!"

James stopped suddenly. "I don't like that."

I put my arm through his. "I have quick reflexes."

"I don't like that at all," James said, drew his arm out from under mine, and placed it tightly around my shoulders. We walked to our cars.

Thirty Three

We both had parked behind a storage shed in the La Montanita Coop parking lot. I unlocked the door to my VW Beetle and tossed in my purse. I turned to say good-bye. James put his hands on my waist. I ran a finger down his tie.

"Don't touch it unless you mean it, Mrs. Steele."

I pulled his tie.

"I warned you." We fell against the Bug. He lifted me up against him. I threw the car keys over my shoulder. I grabbed his hair. I tried to wrap both legs around his waist. One slid to the ground. The other stayed up. But we swayed. I was going down. Damn! How did they do this in the movies? Skinny actors. I pushed against the car with one hand. James stopped my fall with his knee. With great strength James hauled me upright. We burst out laughing. Again.

"Hello, Mom."

Max! James and I moved apart. "What are you doing here?" I demanded in my strict mother voice that has never affected one child or student. I saw our dog Suki on a leash. James knelt down to pet her. She wagged her tail.

"I'm walking the dog, Mom. Hi, Inspector Hutchinson."

"Hello Max."

"What in the hell are you doing walking the dog at this hour!"

"Language, Mom. I am getting fresh air."

"Get in the car. We're going home."

"Whatever you say."

"Thank you, Inspector Hutchinson…for coffee," I said.

"You're welcome, Mrs. Steele. Drive safely. Bye, Max."

"Good-bye. Good to see you," Max said.

We got in the car. I slammed the door shut. I glared at Max. James knocked on the window. He held up my keys.

***

We drove in silence for five blocks to our house. Max was really starting to get on my nerves. How did he get so sneaky? But then what am I? I'm done. I'm overdone. I turned off the car.

"Dad has been drinking. He's upset about something." Max said.

"Sad," I said as I opened the garage door. Suki jumped out the window.

"I thought you two had made up."

"I don't know what is going through his mind, Max, and I don't care."

"You don't care?"

"I don't care."

"Well, I care that you don't care."

I hugged him tightly. "Oh, Max, I love you." He hugged me back.

"I love you, too, Mom." I started crying. "Are you leaving Dad?"

"I don't know."

"For the Inspector?"

"I don't know."

"Let's go inside. You must be tired after the museum opening, eating a Napoleon with the Inspector, and then visiting Mariposa." Max grinned.

"I give up," I sighed.

"Don't ever do that, Mom!"

***

John was sitting in his Finnish chair staring at a soccer game on a Spanish Channel. His eyes were slits. Slowly blinking like a lizard. His mouth was a small, wrinkled prune. The closed up den stank of stale wine and nicotine breath. I stood there. He never looked at me. Asshole. I went into our bedroom to change into my comfy clothes. I saw a dirty, wrinkled piece of paper stabbed with a corkscrew on my pillow. Oh God. And that was my favorite pillow. I even packed it on trips. I sat on the bed. It was the note. The wind swept note. John's note. I took the corkscrew out of my pillow and removed the note. I straightened the torn, stained paper. I shook my head as I tried to re-read the note. Only fragments were legible: "…starving…love…don't ever…my dear…beautiful…body…desire…"

What morose, sentimental slop, I thought again. Or was it? What was I turning into?

I jammed the note back on the corkscrew and brought it into the den. I held it in front of John's lowered, slack, dozing face.

I said loudly, "A little dramatic, wouldn't you say?"

John woke up. He raised his head. After he focused his bleary eyes, he started slurring. "Shannon got an eye-full when she found that in her back yard. Did you throw it away? The outpouring of my soul? My heart? My feelings treated like garbage?"

"Stop it. I read your note outside on the deck. I put it on the table. The wind blew it away. That's all," I said.

"You don't love me anymore."

"You need to go to bed."

Douglas and Max came into the den.

"Come on, Dad," Douglas said. He and Max stood by John's chair.

John slowly stood up. "Off you go," I said like talking to a child.

My sons led him out.

"Your mother doesn't love me anymore," I heard John mutter.

I opened the windows. The fragrant night air caressed my face.

Thirty Four

I tore the tattered note up and threw it in the outside trashcan. I tossed the corkscrew back in the junk drawer. I poured a glass of wine and took a long, hot bath. Then I sat on the back deck with another glass and lit a cigarette. I did not know what to do. I was not going to get in that bed with John. Max and Douglas came out to kiss me good-night. I told them that I was all right. I thanked them. I loved them. I walked back inside, rummaged around the linen closet. What a disaster of stringy wadded up thermal blankets, ragged comforters, old duvet covers, thin beach towels, and torn sheets. If I died suddenly and someone went through my linens, they'd be shocked. Shabby chic. No…not chic…plain shabby. (But she dressed so well, they'd exclaim!) That's me. My true inner life was hidden from view like the linens: knotted grief, worn out regrets, ancient fears, faded dreams… all crammed onto shelves of paralyzing ambivalence. I pulled out an Urban Outfitters blanket covered with dangling sequins and beads. I went into our bedroom, grabbed my punctured pillow, another pillow, and the gray knit poncho my mother gave me when I was pregnant with Peter kept in the lower chest drawer next to my side of the bed. John was snoring away. The whole room smelled of his fetid breath. When I plopped down on our $3,000 couch in the den, I bumped into my dog curled up in the middle. Suki gave me a gimlet eye and moved to the end of the couch.

"Sorry to disturb you, Your Majesty," I said. She closed her eyes. I wished I were a dog. I covered myself with the soft, fringed poncho. I felt my mother's love even though she had been dead for 17 years.

I stared into the darkness for a while. Chopstick sounds came from somewhere. A text? I checked my phone. Nothing. I turned on the light. John's phone was on the coffee table. I picked it up. I read: I am here 4 U. Alice! I punched in his security code and checked his text messages. There were no others from her. I looked at his recent phone calls: two from Alice tonight. Not to mention phone calls going out to her number in days past. Well. Maybe she'll take him away and do something with him. On that thought I tucked my feet under Suki's warm body, closed my eyes and fell immediately to sleep.

Thirty Five

The water caressed my skin. The first chill I felt diving into the pool changed into an exhilarating coolness that I felt throughout my body. My hot, angry feelings melted away. I swam. And swam. Up and down the lap lane. Each stroke gave me strength. Each stroke soothed my fevered thoughts. Every kick banished anger. I felt weightless and free. For a while. Oh water. Thank you.

But when I changed over to my lazy side stroke and back stroke, reality rushed in. Even though I tried to concentrate on the colorful pennants waving above me, the big clock on the wall, the blue buoys floating on the lane dividers, my thoughts went back again to John. I thought of the cartoon on my bulletin board that has delighted me for years...in a sick way: Two women are walking arm and arm down a busy downtown street. One is saying to the other: "I feel so much better now that I'm back in denial." I started laughing just thinking about it. It was so me. But I swallowed some water and started choking. I stopped at the end of the lane, coughed and rubbed my bloodshot eyes. The lifeguard was looking at me. I started to swim again. No more denial. The facts. Only the facts. Face my problems instead of running away. Tomorrow. For sure.

I got to the other end of the lane, hoisted myself up and out, and walked to the open swim part of the Olympic Pool. I eased in and started a dead man's float on my back. I was a starfish. I thought about what I had to do today. Bring some museum shop merchandise downtown to Pat. What should I bring? A few books, some jewelry, some cards…I was doing it again! Distracting myself! I flipped over on my stomach. I felt like a jellyfish. Probably looked like one, too.

How do I handle this? When John acted like nothing weird happened this morning! Did he have a black out? He must have. I was speechless when he came in the den early this morning after Douglas had left for band practice.

"Are you sick?" he asked.

Of you, I wanted to say, but I instead I said no.

"Why did you sleep out here?"

"Because you freaked me out last night."

"I did?"

"John! You stabbed your note on my favorite pillow with a corkscrew!"

"Oh that…I didn't mean to scare you. I was just surprised and hurt when the neighbor brought it over. I'll buy you a new pillow."

"Do you remember what I said to you about the note?"

"Umm…something about the wind?"

"Forget it." I went in our bedroom, gagged at the funky smell, lit a candle, opened the windows and quickly crammed my Lady of Guadalupe bag with a swimming suit, towel, soap, make-up and work clothes.

John watched me. "Oh honey…come here…" He opened his arms.

"Don't," I walked out of the room.

"Where are you going this early? You haven't had coffee. I made coffee. Hey! I was hurt! Now I understand! Hey!"

I went into the kitchen. I kissed Max on the head while he was foraging in the refrigerator. He pulled out a box of leftover pizza. "Have a good day, Mom," he said.

***

I stood up in the pool, took a deep breath, sunk down and swam under water to the far edge like a mermaid. I wished I were a mermaid. I rested my head up on the side of the pool, kicked my legs, and watched swimmers going in and out. Where was my Inspector?

Thirty Six

I drove west down Central Avenue to the 516 University Art Museum satellite located downtown. Good old Historic Route 66. Too scenic for words. When I passed under the railroad tracks, I saw my "neighborhood" movie theatre Century 14 on the corner of 1st and Central. Across from the Railroad Station. I saw the Rail Runner stopped for passengers with the Red Road Runner on the side. I liked riding that up to Santa Fe. The movie theatre was the last decent building before a long stretch of sleazy, low class bars, the decrepit, rather sinister looking Sunshine Theatre which amazingly still booked popular musical artists, and shabby homeless shuffling along the sidewalks. Second, Third, Fourth Streets were eyesores on both sides. 516 was located between 5th and 6th streets. Oh what was Roland thinking of! What kind of visitors came downtown to look at art? Crazy. Poor Pat! I drove past the gallery to public parking at the end of 8th street. At least that was across from a beautiful park.

I walked down to 516 with my box of merchandise that no one will probably buy. At least this block had some class. But I still smelled puke and urine. To my left at the end of the next block was the Historic Kimo Theatre. The Pueblo Indian Deco structure was built in the early 1920s. I had gone to film festivals and music concerts there over the years. I loved the animal skulls on the walls with tiny white lights showing through the eye sockets. But these performances were at night. And 516 will be closed at night. What a disastrous plan. But I was here to help.

I crossed 6th street. I ignored an obnoxious beggar. He cursed me. Welcome to downtown Albuquerque. I saw Pat hosing down the sidewalk. "Pat! What are you doing?" I walked quickly towards her.

"Washing off the entryway. There were puddles of pee and someone took a dump in front of the door!"

"Oh Pat! I am so sorry! Can you call the city? They should handle this!"

Pat put her thumb over the spout of an old green hose to make the water spray out with more force. She blasted the disgusting refuse into the gutter. Then she aimed the stream to obliterate every trace left in the street in front of the gallery. "This is not in my job description!"

"You have to tell Roland!"

"I talked to Richard Levy next door. He has to do this himself all the time. "

"Still not right!"

"I'm OK, Caro...just go inside and display your pretty wares."

"Hahaha! They will fly out of the gallery, I'm sure!"

The inside of the 516 was like walking into a cool, clean, spare space naturally lit from the front floor to ceiling glass windows. High ceilings, white walls, black and white art deco tile on the floors. A long staircase with a black banister led up to a second floor. I loved it! Large Polaroid portrait photographs by Miguel Gandert hung in the front part of the first floor. What a visual hook! A partial, low half wall separated the main floor in two airy spaces. I walked toward the back section of the gallery and saw more photographs by Betty Hahn, Clinton Adams, and Juliet Margaret Cameron--hung where they were out of the sunlight--a few wild Raymond Jonson modern explosions, some landscapes and a fiberglass sculpture by Luis Jimenez. There was a bathroom and small kitchen near the rear steel, padlocked door.

I have to admit that I never read labels in museums, but I wandered around seeing who painted the unfamiliar landscapes. I read one next to a painting of low, soft brown mesas framed by a beautiful blue sky above and muted spring flowers below entitled *Rancho Encantada*. Charles Lowry. I went to another painting of a moon coming over a mountain called *Ghost Moon*. Charles Lowry. Damn! I moved on to a long, narrow painting of vivid white hollyhocks entitled *Female Ambition*. What?

Pat joined me after she washed her hands. "So the Art Museum owns Charles's art?" I asked.

"Well...he didn't leave any heirs. These and others were found unframed in his office in the Art and Art History Building. The titles were on the back."

"Finders keepers...I guess."

We walked to the front.

"So what is upstairs?" I asked.

"Spanish Colonial."

"As it should be," I said. Pat laughed.

"I made a space on a table for some merchandise. I have a small amount of cash and a credit card machine."

"Thank you, Pat." I arranged a few art books, a colorful bowl of silver rings, and a few sacred heart tee shirts on a white table. I stacked some art reproduction postcards in a narrow, long basket. I put a receipt book in Pat's desk drawer. "Have you had many visitors?

"Four yesterday. Woohoo! Roland thinks that after our big opening next week, word will get out. Richard Levy's gallery has been in business for a long time. So there's hope! And a lot of tourists shop at Skip Maisel's Indian Jewelry two doors down...We'll see...Are you hungry?"

Pat called in a carry-out order of two BLTs and fries to Lindy's on the corner of 5th and Central, and I picked it up. The waitress called me honey when I walked in. Now those Greeks seemed nice! Not like the screaming crew at Olympia restaurant near the university. But Greeks were rather bipolar. Not like Macedonians--my people. We were the epitome of sanity and stability-- the poster race for mental health.

After lunch I had to get back to the main Art Museum. Then I had to go home. I got in my car, screamed, honked the horn, beat on the steering wheel and burst into tears.

Thirty Seven

I was closing out the credit card machine right before the museum closed at 4:00 when Roland walked in twirling his tennis racquet. I stopped what I was doing. But I remained seated. No more bouncing up trying to please. He stood in front of the desk, did not greet me, shoved his racquet under one arm, and started humming while picking through silver rings I had on display in a pottery bowl. Silence. He took one ring out and slipped it on his little finger. He wagged it in front of my face.

"I always know Olive's ring size. It's the same as my little finger," he said.

"How handy." He glared at me. "For buying the right gift," I said.

"Yeah...so how are you, Caro?" he asked. He pulled the ring off and tossed it back in the bowl.

"Fine, thank you. How are you?"

"I'm a little disturbed. You see…Caro…when Olive, my wife, is unhappy, everyone is unhappy."

"Really."

"Oh yes, dear Caro, really."

Silence. I held his gaze, but my heart was pounding. I was alone. The museum was empty. He came around the front desk and stood over me.

"So when you come into her space with a policeman, confront her with her history with Charles, insinuate that her assistants are somehow, shall we say, untrustworthy dropouts, she gets really mad. And she tells me. And then I get really mad that my Museum Shop Manager is joined at the hip to a policeman and sticking her nose into matters that don't concern her one little bit."

I stood up. Roland did not move back.

"Olive insulted me, Roland, and threatened me. Are you threatening me, too?"

"Hear this, dear Caro, if I hear from Olive that you ever come near her again, you will be out of a job."

"Gee whiz! What will I ever do? I'll have to go outside and shoot myself!"

He grabbed my upper arm. I saw the sweat beads on his forehead. I smelled his sweat. He clenched his teeth.

"I may save you the trouble…" he hissed.

"So the museum is still open? It's after 4." My Inspector walked through the open doors. Rowland swiftly moved his hand up to my shoulder and patted it. I shrugged him off. My legs went weak, but I stayed standing. I looked at Roland with a closed mouth smile.

"I was just telling our Caro to close up. She works too hard. So dedicated. And how are you, James?" Roland sprinted around the desk and shook James's hand. He turned back to me and boomed. "What would we ever do without her? Inconceivable!" He walked out the door swishing his racquet to and fro.

James watched Roland leave. He turned around. "Roland dresses really well to play on campus courts. Fila chevron polo and Essenza shorts? Does he think he's at Wimbledon? Who's he trying to impress around here?" He laughed.

Silence.

"Mrs. Steele?"

My bloodshot eyes filled with tears.

Thirty Eight

James rushed to me. "Are you all right? What happened? What's wrong with your eyes?"

I collapsed in my chair. I reached for his hands. "Roland said Olive was upset with me. He squeezed my arm and threatened me! I swam without goggles, then I cried."

"Son of a bitch!" James said.

"Why are you here, James?" I gripped his hands tighter.

"Making arrangements with charming Clarence to bolt cut lockers open tomorrow. But now I want to know exactly what happened to you!"

I started crying and pressed his hand to my cheek.

James freed himself from my vise-like grip, closed the museum door, and turned off the Museo Art Museum sign. He raised my wet noodle body off the chair and led me through the book room into the storage closet.

He propped me up against the shelves, ran out and rolled in a chair. He shut the door, sat down, and pulled me onto his lap. I curled up in his arms. He cradled me like a child. I boo-hooed into his neck. He rubbed my back.

"I've had a hard day," I said.

"I'm sorry, Mrs. Steele...What did Roland say to you?"

"I had to stay away from Olive, or I'd lose my job. I made some snarky remark about doing myself in with despair, and he said that he might save me the trouble."

"He'll regret that. I don't want you to ever be alone with him again. And I want you to stay away from Olive."

I hiccupped. James gave me his handkerchief.

"Do you hear me?" he said.

"Yes," I whispered into his fresh-smelling, if rather soggy by now, green plaid shirt. I wanted to snuffle there forever.

"Will you listen to me...for once? Let me do my job?"

"But..." James turned my body towards him. I lifted one leg over his lap. I faced him. I put my hands on his shoulders. I lost myself in his beautiful eyes.

"No buts, OK?" he said. I nodded yes. "...So you swam today?"

"Yes." I kissed him.

"And the chlorine burned your eyes." He kissed me

"Yes." I kissed him.

"And you cried because I wasn't at the pool?" James said with a smile.

"No!" I laughed.

"Then why?"

"My life is changing. I'm scared."

"Don't be afraid, Mrs. Steele."

I put my arms around his neck.

The office chair slowly rolled back and forth over the tiled floor.

Thirty Nine

I pulled into the garage with a box of Golden Pride Chicken. I kept licking my tender lips. Tasting my Inspector again. I had a moment. Just with his mouth on mine.

Douglas ran out.

"For the love of God please make him stop!" he said before I even got out of the car.

"What's going on?"

"Dad keeps making Chinese food! He's frying every vegetable grown on the planet earth in tempera batter! And he hasn't even started on fried rice!"

I walked into the laundry room. The house was filled with smoke and smelled of burnt oil.

"He's set off the smoke alarm! I had to disconnect it!" Douglas said.

John was standing in front of the stove wearing my St. Martha--A Kitchen Saint apron and holding a slotted spoon in the air. Swirls of smoke came out of the cast iron skillet. The counter top was covered in strangely shaped chopped vegetables of every ilk: yams, peppers, cauliflower, broccoli, snap peas, mushrooms, onions, eggplant…! On the other side of the stove were cookie sheets covered in pale fried mounds pooled in oil. Grease splatters covered the walls and the cabinets. What a mess.

"John!" I yelled over the sound of crackling, popping oil. "What are you doing?"

"Caro! I am making dinner! I pulled out my cookbook from my old Chinese Cooking class and said to myself: I will surprise my Caro! I went to Sprouts and shopped for happy vegetables for my family."

"Thank you, John, but you've already made enough here to feed an army. I brought some chicken. Why don't we eat what you've already made…with the chicken?"

"But I cut up all these vegetables! I've been on my feet all afternoon! I took off work! I want to make fried rice!"

"I'll roast them tomorrow. You love roasted vegies! I bought potato salad. We'll have rice another night. It's getting late. The boys are hungry. Now turn off the heat, open some windows…I'll bag the beautifully cut, happy produce. Thank you for preparing them!"

"I wanted to surprise you, Caro," John said all emotional.

"You certainly did! Can't wait to eat your tempura!" I gushed. Placating him, as usual. Never mind the night before. What night before? What corkscrew?

What secretary? Let's forget about the whole episode and eat and drink and smoke. Be happy! Look how much I do for you!

"I wanted you to come home to us and relax," he said.

"I will! But I have to take off my bra."

Max and Douglas met me in the hall both talking at once: "Suki is under my bed! Dad is a maniac--He did not let us in the kitchen--He did not listen to us--I'm not eating that soggy stuff--Thank you for the chicken--I will eat outside--The house stinks."

I gathered them both in a group hug.

"Let's just eat calmly. Your Dad has worked very hard."

"Your mouth's all swollen, Mom," Douglas said.

"Had kale salad for lunch. Bad allergic reaction."

"Classic!" Max said.

Forty

"Are you going to bed?" John asked.

"Not right now. I have to read more of Tina's book. We're meeting next week."

"Don't sleep rob, honey." He bent to kiss me. I turned my head. His lips grazed my cheek.

"Oh don't worry!" I chirped and walked out of our bedroom into the den.

I leaned back against the pillows on the couch, pulled the spangled Urban Outfitter blanket over me, opened the heavy *Cinnamon Summer* manuscript, and tucked my feet under Suki's warm belly. I did not know how long I could keep my eyes opened, but I was not getting into bed with John tonight. Or any other night. Maybe.

I had finally washed the greasy film off my skin and out of my hair. The house still smelled of oily smoke--even with all the windows and doors open. The boys and I cleaned up the kitchen. Took us an hour. John fell asleep in his Finnish chair immediately after we ate--too much wine while cooking and too much wine with dinner. He woke up after I had my bath. I was sitting on our bed staring when he came into the room. I mentally thanked my friend Tina for sharing her work with me: A perfect excuse for an exit.

OK, where was I? Oh yeah…Lily made a cake. With cinnamon! I saw a connection here. I read:

I'll be glad to leave Chance to finish his wiring or whatever and move on to work somewhere else. If I never see him again it would be too soon, Lily grumbled to herself. Now that she was awake and in the light of day, she thought more clearly. The more she remembered how he took advantage of her and touched her 'down there' and his awful, rude dog, her white straight teeth ground together. She did not like feeling out of control. But she had control of her baking! Inside Geneva's house, she cut the remaining apple cake into squares, wrapped them in plastic wrap and used some colorful string tied to the doorknob of her Aunt's laundry room. She emptied a wicker basket filled with clothes pins, put in the brightly wrapped pieces of apple cake, and set off toward town.

(To Grandmother's house we go.)

Lily felt a wave of happiness through her body. She kicked off her Havaianas. She started walking lazily over the beautifully manicured lawns. The lush, thick grass felt so good between her toes. Not one cigarette butt or dog poop. No empty fast food containers. No beer bottles or used rubbers. No trash! At all! She saw a flower growing out of a crack in the sidewalk. Lily picked the small orange blossom, and stuck it behind her ear.

Lily took deep breaths of the sea air. She watched all the boats in the bay and the large ferries moving between the tips of Long Island.

Lily slipped on her flip-flops when she turned onto Main Street. She saw a big ice-cream cone sign. It was attached to a small white house. She walked gracefully up the steps to the large front porch and opened the screen door. A bell rang.

(She needed a red hooded cape.)

The aroma of freshly brewed coffee greeted her. Such a cheerful shop! White eyelet curtains hung at the windows. Red geraniums in vividly colored ceramic pots lined the window sills. Two canaries sang sweetly from a large bird cage. Round white bistro tables and chairs were placed around the airy room.

A tall, well-fed middle-aged woman appeared from a back room. She stood behind the ice-cream freezer case. She had frizzy red hair done up in a high pony tail, wore a blue striped maxi-dress covered with pink checked apron. She wore red Crocs.

"Yes?" she said in a deep voice.

"Hello," Lily said. "My name is Lily Barnett. I am staying with my Aunt…"

"I know, honey. Geneva's been talking about you coming for days. Welcome to Greenport! I'm Flo. Let's sit and have coffee."

Flo poured coffee for them both in translucent china floral cups with saucers. She placed a small robin egg's blue pottery pitcher of cream and matching bowl of raw sugar cubes on the table. Lily felt immediately at ease with Flo's practical, no nonsense manner.

"Now," Flo said looking at the wicker basket. "What did you bring me?"

"Apple cake. Aunt Geneva said you should taste it. She wants you start selling baked goods again."

"That you make?"

"Well, yes." Lily blushed bright pink.

"Hmmm." Flo winked at her and smiled. She unwrapped a piece of cake and took a big bite. "Delicious, Lily! Why don't you bring me a few baked goods first thing in the morning the rest of the week. I'll see how it goes."

"You've got a deal."

The screen door crashed open. Chance ran in. He stopped. His body blocked the morning sun, but shards of light shone around and through his long hair. Like a halo. Or a flaming aura. He wore cut-off jeans, a black muscle shirt, and black Converse tennis shoes. The lavender scented hoodie was tied around his neck. Lily froze.

(The big bad wolf. Thank goodness.)

"Why, Chance! Hello, honey..." Flo said.

"I need your car!" Chance shouted.

Flo stood up. "Why? What happened?"

"I can't explain. I've got to leave Greenport!"

"Why?" Flo cried.

"Can't explain now! The police are looking for me! I didn't do anything!"

Flo ran to a drawer, took out some keys and threw them across the room to Chance.

(She trusts the wolf!)

He caught the keys with one hand and lifted Lily out of her chair with the other. "You're coming with me!"

"No!" Lily screamed.

"Yes!" Chance shouted. He put his arm around her waist and carried her like a sack of potatoes out the door. The flower in her hair fell on the steps. Lily kicked her legs furiously, but Chance held her tightly.

"Help!" she screamed again. Only the dogs tied to a tree heard her. They wagged their tails.

Flo stood on the porch with her hand over her mouth.

"Go to Geneva's! Now!" Chance hollered.

Flo started running down the street.

Chance unlocked the Fiat 500 and shoved Lily in the front seat. She tried to get out, but he locked the doors. Chance picked up her orange flower and untied the dogs. They jumped in the back seat and started licking Lily. Chance raced around to the driver's side, slid in, gently placed the flower behind Lily's ear, inserted the key and took off. Lily leaned over and started pounding on his chest.

"Stop! Let me out!"

"I will tie you up if I have to! Now buckle up for safety!"

"How dare you, you…"

Chance swerved to a stop, reached in back, unhooked the Bruno's dog leash, and tied Lily's hands together.

(Oh Tina…was Chance into bondage? I hoped not.)

She struggled but to no avail. Chance reached over her to pull down the seat belt; His body pressed over hers. Lily felt that odd feeling again between her legs. His body so close to hers was quite overwhelmingly delicious. Chance had such energy. He electrified her. Like she was connected to the mysteries of the universe. Life force at last! Chance clicked her seat belt in place. Suddenly, Lily had the strong urge to lean over and kiss his neck. But she didn't.

(Bite him! I paused to remember when my Inspector bit my finger. Gently. Surprisingly. I sucked on my finger as I read on.)

"Animal!" she said weakly.

He untied his sweat shirt from around his neck, threw it in the back seat, and pulled off his wife-beater. "I'll stuff this in your mouth if you don't shut up!"

Lily got silent. Chance peeled off.

Her heart was pounding. She had to think. She started to take deep breaths: In through her nose, hold for five counts, out through her mouth. She was a reed. Her heart slowed but then began to soar as she stared at his handsome profile, lean chest and bare, well-formed thighs. Lily suddenly had a wild vision of licking his legs! The opened windows made his long hair blow wildly. Lily felt thrilled to be tied up in this car with Chance. She shook her curls. Snap out of it, she thought.

(Please don't. I can't.)

Chance noticed the car was out of gas. He pulled into Robert's gas station and filled up. Lily sat quietly. She looked at her tied hands with the loose knot. She could easily free herself but instead slowly turned the silver lapis azuli ring that she bought at the airport in New Orleans around and around her finger. Lily felt so happy there. She and Brad went to clubs, but Brad drank so much that he went to sleep sitting up before the dancing started. She would sit on the hotel balcony after Brad passed out in a chair and watch the lively French Quarter scene. The music floating over the city thrilled her. She felt alone but alive.

Then Lila stared lovingly at the Art Carved pear-shaped diamond ring set in platinum: her mother's engagement ring. She still missed her sweet mother who died in a car accident ten years before. Lily thought about her wedding ring that she'd left on the dressing table in Dallas. She often developed an itchy rash under the heavy gold band. Should have taken that as a sign, she thought. Lily was jolted back to the present when Chance yanked open the car door and turned on the ignition. She liked the present she thought surprisingly.

They drove in silence over the causeway into Orient. They passed through sparse, clean, white houses, perfectly manicured lawns, a general store, a red brick elementary school, a small fire station, and a working gas station right out of the 1950s. He turned onto a road that steeply dropped to a rocky ledge. He stopped, turned the car off, and got out. He opened the back door for the dogs and grabbed his sweatshirt. Bruno and Tulip ran joyfully down the rocky hill. Chance opened the passenger door, and unsnapped Lily's seat belt. She loved it when he leaned over her again. His body radiated heat. And promise. She wanted more. He untied her hands.

"Was that too tight?" he asked.

"No... What are you going to do to me?"

(I can only hope.)

 "Taking you to Secret Beach."

"What?"

Chance led her carefully over huge rocks down to the water where the rocks became tiny pebbles. Lily stumbled in her flip-flops.

"Give me those!" he said. Lily held onto his well-formed shoulders as he removed her shoes. She actually navigated the large smooth stones much better with bare feet. They came at last to a small sandy beach near the ocean.

Chance laid his sweatshirt on the ground. "Sit," he said.

Lily sat. She was so scared now. There was no one within sight. How could this man cause such extreme feelings in her? She was on a roller coaster of emotions! What was he going to do to her? And, more disturbing to think about, would she like it?

(Oh please! Spare me this angst!)

Tulip was frolicking in the ocean with Bruno. Some protector!!!

"I went to your Aunt's house," Chance said as he sat down beside her. "I was worried because Tulip was running loose around the neighborhood when I came to work on your cottage. I heard a male voice yelling: 'Where is Lily? You better tell me, you old bat!' Screams. I burst through the door. Geneva was on the floor."

"Oh my God!" Lily cried.

"Blood running from her head. A man was standing over her. He saw me, tackled me, and went out the front door. I crawled over to Geneva and held her head."

"Was she dead?" Lily screamed.

"Unconscious. Steady pulse. I called 911 on my cell phone. I got up to get a wet cloth. I passed the screen door where the mailman was standing with a package.

He shouted 'What have you done now, Chance'?" I yelled "nothing', but he saw the blood on my hands and pulled out his cell phone. I had to leave, Lily."

"I've got to see my aunt!" Lily stood up.

"Stay away. Someone is after you," Chance said.

"Oh my God! Who?"

"Tall, blonde, muscular with a Texas accent."

(Oh my God. Brad.)

"Oh my God! Brad!" Lily started to cry. Chance jumped up. He held her close. She clung to him.

He gently lowered her to the ground as she continued to sob into his warm chest.

"Who's Brad?"

Well, well, well...The plot is thickening nicely. I turned out the light. I thought about my Inspector's chest all warm and wet from my tears. I will not be afraid of tomorrow. "Here is now, isn't it girl?" I whispered. Suki licked my hand.

Forty One

"Mom! Can I take your car today?

I opened my eyes. "What?" Douglas was standing over me.

"My car won't start! I have to be at the battle of the bands at Eldorado High School in 30 minutes!"

John walked in the den. "Use my car. Your mother can take me to work."

"No! He can have my car. I'll take the bus to work." I said still flat on my back.

"Thanks, Mom!" Douglas ran out the front door. I sat up and rubbed my eyes. It was 6:30 AM. John was staring at me.

"Must have been a good book, Caro."

"Yes. Tina's outdone herself. I read and read and fell right asleep."

"Are you going to make a habit of this?"

"What do you mean?"

"Are you going to sleep with me again?"

"Are you going to look at Douglas's car?"

Suki jumped off the couch. I got up, squeezed past a looming John, and let her outside. I walked into the kitchen. He followed me. I poured a little cream in a cup and warmed it in the microwave. I felt John's eyes boring into the back of my head. I took the cup out and poured myself some coffee. I got the Rediwhip out of the frig. I swirled some on top of my coffee. I put the cream back. I took a slow sip of coffee. I turned to him.

"Douglas needs his car, John," I said.

"And I need you."

"You need Alice."

"What the fuck are you talking about?"

Max stumbled past us and opened the refrigerator. "Please!" he said. He took out a leftover fried chicken drumstick. He plopped down in a chair and started reading the *Albuquerque Journal*. I poured him a glass of orange juice and left the kitchen. John followed me into the den and closed the door.

"Are you crazy?" John said.

"I saw texts and calls between you and Alice on your phone two nights ago. I'm not crazy.

"You...," John said. His face got red. "You don't understand." He moved close to my face.

I did not step back. "Well, she does. What a comfort, I'm sure. Excuse me. I have to get dressed and catch a bus."

"What's happened to you, Caro?"

"Something good, John."

Forty Two

I walked down Central Avenue a few blocks to the bus stop in front of the 7-11. I joined a colorful group of people. They all looked like they had come straight out of bed: plaid flannel pants, baggy shorts, stained shirts, Crocs, stocking caps with little puff balls on the top. A woman was flossing her teeth, a man was eating a 7-11 breakfast sandwich with a Big Gulp, and another man was muttering to himself while waving a lit cigarette. I stood primly by holding my sack lunch in one hand and the correct change in another. My Manhattan Portage bag was slung across my chest. No one spoke. Where were these people going? A mystery.

I found a seat near a window. A very old man moved from the seat behind me to the empty one beside me. He smiled. I smiled. Thank goodness I had a short trip down to the university. Public transportation on Central was another world.

"What do you have in your sack?" he asked.

"My lunch," I said.

"What did you make?"

"Turkey sandwich, chips, and a Diet Coke."

"Yum...But have you found Jesus?"

"Oh yes."

"Are you sure?"

"I am very sure," I said and nodded my head gravely. I was almost there. Thank you, Jesus.

"The rapture is coming. Don't want to be left behind!"

"No way!" I said. I reached up to push the buzzer. "My stop! Have a good day!"

"Peace of the Lord be always with you!"

"And also with you!" I squeezed past his bony legs and blessedly stepped off the bus.

***

As I walked through the foyer to the Art Museum I saw my Inspector and Lt. Keyes talking to Clarence in front of the Theatre office. Clarence was holding a bolt cutter almost as big as he was. I fought a huge urge to join them, but I had to check in. The museum door was already opened. Cathy sat at the front desk. I put my purse in the back closet. I rolled the office chair back to the front desk.

"Why was that in there?" Cathy asked.

"I have no idea," I said. "I'm going to put my lunch in the office frig."

I opened the administrative office's door with my key. Roland's door was opened. The three others were shut, of course. I couldn't see Linda behind her sky high cubicle walls. The little refrigerator was in the corner of the entryway. I stuffed my bag in and turned around. Roland was leaning against the front door.

"I saw that policeman talking to Clarence," he said.

I just looked at him.

"Any idea why?" he asked.

"I have no idea," I said. "Excuse me." I reached around him for the doorknob. He stepped too close to me, put his hand over mine and squeezed.

"I think you do, Caro." For the second time this morning I had to look up into another looming male tense face--another man pressing his body and point with me in a most uncomfortable way. Another man invading my personal space. To hell with them, I thought. I've had it!

Linda came lumbering around the corner. I was never so glad to see anyone in my life. Of all people! Roland quickly stepped away from me.

"I've got to talk to you about a security lapse, Caro!" she said.

"Really? I am so sorry! Let's go down to the museum, and you can tell me everything. I can't wait to know! I care!"

"Hurrumph," she said.

Linda barged between me and Roland, opened the door, and I followed her out.

"Sunday we had a report that your student helpers were laughing and talking so loudly that it disturbed a guest."

"I have to check to see who was on duty. I will have a talk with them."

"You better! Also I have to show you how to reset the alarm on the door going into the Coke Gallery. Again… one of your Sunday crew let a person in a wheelchair in and then forgot reset the alarm! A custodian reported to the Dean that he unlocked the door to get in to clean, and the alarm didn't go off. The campus police came. Huge disturbance, Caro!"

"I never knew about that door's alarm."

I followed Linda through the art museum to the side gallery door. Cathy mouthed a silent "what?" as we passed by. I gave her a thumbs up.

"Here is the black box. Always put the lever back down after you close this door."

"Ok. Now I know. Again, I am so sorry." I had to get down to the lockers with my Inspector! When will this ever end?

"Well, Pat should have told you. And, actually, I should have also. Don't let it happen again!"

"Don't worry. I won't. And thank you, Linda!" I said with a big smile. I almost shook her hand.

She squinted her eyes and looked at me. "You're welcome, Caro." She walked away. I heard her mutter "What the fuck?"

***

I rushed to the front desk. I asked Cathy if she had to take a break before I left "for an important errand in the basement". She said she was fine and that Mike was coming in to relieve her soon. I shot out the museum doors, flew around the corner and ran down the stairs. I walked briskly down the narrow hallway lined with lockers and closed classroom doors to the Men's Dressing Room. The door was propped open. I walked in. My Inspector and Lt. Jane Keyes were facing the double row of lockers against one wall. Clarence was snipping the locks off one by one. This took a lot of strength. I stood quietly against the sagging rubber curtain that hung in front of the shower. Stained urinals and one toilet stall were against one wall and a mirror hung over a long dressing table with chairs against the other wall.

"This is not going to be pleasant," Clarence said. "Breathe through your mouth!"

James and Jane put on latex gloves. I wished I had a pair! He opened a locker. It was filled with newspapers. He opened another packed with smelly underwear, a bottle of vodka fell out of another and crashed to the floor.

"Great!" Clarence said. He ran out. James watched him go and saw me.

"Mrs. Steele. What a pleasant surprise."

"Indeed. Hi Jane."

"Hello, Caro." She looked at James then back at me. Silence.

"I'm the one who told Inspector Hutchinson that Charles had a locker here," I said. Like I had to explain my presence to her?

Clarence came back lugging a broom, mop and a dustpan. Leroy walked behind him with a bucket of sudsy water.

"Leroy! What are you doing here?" I asked.

"Helping, Little Missy! Cathy told me you went down to the basement. And who are these fine people?"

Jane frowned and whispered something to James. I had to say: "And Leroy is the one who told me about Charles's locker." So there.

While I made introductions, Clarence swept up glass and threw it in the trash can. He started mopping the floor. "I'm waiting!" he snapped at Leroy. Leroy kept talking to my Inspector.

"Look in number 37," he said.

Clarence stopped and held up the dripping mop. "Well! Thanks for telling us now! A blister has just erupted on my palm from squeezing the bolt cutter." He held up a lily white, small, perfectly manicured hand. "You think that's funny..."

"I just got here! Take a chill pill, Clarence!"

"Have another drink, you..."

"Let's go!" James said.

We gathered around while Jane opened the locker 37. Little shelves had been installed that held soap, shampoo, nail clippers, a razor, a small framed photo of a smiling woman, and a roll of toilet paper. James took each item out and placed them on the dressing table. The locker was empty. What a bust!

Jane took the photo out of its frame. She read the back out loud: "Anne in El Morrow 2010".

"Roland's wife," Leroy said. "Ex-wife, actually."

We all stared at him.

The roll of toilet paper fell off the table. I leaned over to pick it up but had no gloves! Did not want to contaminate evidence! I saw something inside its cardboard cylinder, though.

"There is an object stuffed in the middle," I said and pointed to the roll.

James picked it up. He reached inside and pulled out a thin paper scroll. He sat down and carefully uncurled it. We all stood around him and looked over his shoulders. There were two tattered pieces of paper with faded typing. He handed one to Jane. (Oh! I thought!) She read it to us as we looked on:

Georgia O'Keeffe 1887-1986
Grey Hill Forms, 1936
Oil on canvas, 20" X 30"
Gift of the Estate of Georgia O'Keeffe
Permanent loan to the University Art Museum
Museum of Fine Arts
87.449.1

James held up the second sheet. We all moved around him as he read:

Georgia O'Keeffe 1887-1986
White Flowers, 1926
Oil on canvas.
From the Estate of Georgia O'Keeffe
87.21.2

"What are these?" Jane asked.
"Copies of Provenance," Leroy said. "I'll be damned…"
"What?" James asked.

"Provenance confirms authenticity in a work of art," Leroy intoned in a professorial voice. "It leaves no doubt that a work of art is genuine and by the artist who's signature it bears. These are copies…of proof of purchase. Someone bought these! So what is in the museum? Are they still in the museum?" He shook his head. "Oh my God…what did my friend do? I need a drink." He lurched out of the dressing room.

James carefully placed the documents in a plastic bag.

"Excuse me, Clarence. Hate to leave you with this mess, but I have to talk to Lt. Keyes. Thank you for your help. I don't want this information to go any further than this room. Understand?"

"Yeah…yeah…my ruby reds are sealed," Clarence muttered sullenly, but he did shake my Inspector's offered hand.

"Bye, Clarence. Thank you," I said.

"Yeah…whatever. I'm just another staff bot!" he said and continued to mop up the vodka.

"So am I, Clarence."

I left to catch up with my Inspector and Jane who were walking slowly down the hall with their heads close together quietly talking. Well, I had something important to say!

Forty Three

"Excuse me," I said. They turned around.

"Yes?" James asked.

"Those Georgia O'Keeffe paintings…They were hanging in the museum before the Graduate Exhibition. I saw them everyday."

"Yes?" Jane said.

"And I've seen some of Charles's work in our downtown satellite museum."

"And?" James said.

"The art is similar."

"What are you trying to say, Caro?" Jane asked.

Before I could answer James walked into the opened doors of Theatre X. The small black box theatre was dark. Only the ghost light was on in the middle of the stage area. He motioned us in. We followed him up to the top row of seats.

"Now, Mrs. Steele. Tell us what you think."

"Why would Charles hide copies of the provenance papers on those two works of art? Unless he had something to do with the art? And they still are in the museum. So he didn't steal them! It doesn't make sense unless he knew a secret involving those particular pieces! Did he copy them? He could have! He had the talent! What if he knew they were copied? And that got him killed?"

My Inspector's phone rang. He answered, got up suddenly, and left Theatre X.

Jane and I sat in silence.

"You're a very observant person, Caro," she finally said. "And you have a vivid imagination."

"Thank you." (I guess, I thought.) I took a deep breath. Where was James? "The Inspector must have had an emergency," I said.

"Could be his wife. You do know he's married, don't you?" Jane said.

"Of course I do."

"And that she's in New Orleans?"

"I know that, Lieutenant Keyes."

"Just wondering, Mrs. Steele."

I stood up. "I have to get back to work."

"Thank you for your keen insights."

I smiled, walked down the rows of chairs and out into the basement hallway.

Back to work my ass, I thought.

Forty Four

I did go back to the art museum. Cathy and Mike were laughing behind the desk. Someone was having fun. I cautioned them about being too loud and explained how to reset the alarm on the Coke Gallery handicapped door. They soberly listened and promised to obey. "Don't worry, Boss," Mike said. I laughed loudly. Too loudly. I was not good boss material. I got a rag out of the infamous back room and started to dust the acrylic cubes full of merchandise in the front window. I saw my Inspector and Jane talking at the entrance to the Fine Arts Center. She left. (Thank God!) James looked down toward the museum. We stared at each other from afar.

"I have to leave for a minute," I said to the students.

"Take your time, Caro! I am making up some hours this afternoon. I'll be here with Mike," Cathy said.

That was all I needed to hear! I grabbed my purse and left. I should have felt guilty about cheating the university. Maybe I can write them a check for $12.50 and pay back my hour salary rate. Or not. James and I walked towards one another. We met in the middle of the foyer. James seemed to look right through me. I felt a fever coming on. We left the Fine Arts Center and walked across to Johnson Center.

"Do you have a locker?" he asked.

"Of course. Do you?"

"Of course."

***

I jumped into the pool with a big splash. My hot body was deliciously chilled. I sprang up next to my Inspector. He was leaning against the side lazily kicking his legs.

"What an entrance, Mrs. Steele."

"I try." I propped my head next to his and slowly kicked my legs, too. "Are you all right, James?"

"I am. All is well…another drama diverted. My wife."

"Your wife."

"Yes, my wife. Monique…is…she has…several times a year she checks herself into a spa…no…more like a clinic."

"A clinic?"

"To sleep…she takes a sleep cure."

"A sleep cure?"

"She needs to rest. She has moments."

"Moments?"

"Needing sleep."

"Is she all right?"

James turned on his stomach. "She ran off with her therapist."

"She woke up?"

"Yes. But they were found, and she's back asleep."

I turned over. I wiped plastered hair out of my eyes. "I'm so sorry."

"Thank you, Mrs. Steele. But she's happier this way."

"My husband sleeps all the time in his Finnish chair."

"Must be something about us," he laughed.

"There's something all right."

James arched back, flipped, and swam underwater to the middle of pool's free space. I followed. I turned over next to him. I wanted to do a dead man's float, but my legs kept sinking. He put his hands under the small of my back. My arms spread wide. My legs rose up. I felt so free.

"Your turn," I said and stood up. James fell back. I put my hands under him. He was so light. I moved on top of him. We smiled at each other with bubbles coming out of our noses as we sank to the bottom. Our hair swirled together. James put his hands around my waist, heaved me up, and tossed me over the water. I screamed. The whistle blew.

We took our towels off the nearby bench and walked out the open doors to the lawn area.

We lay side by side on our towels. We watched dark clouds forming over the Sandia Mountains, but the sun was still shining. The grass was soft and fragrant. I was floating. On solid ground.

James sat up. "I don't want you going near O'Keeffe works at the art museum. I don't want Roland to suspect we know anything about those paintings."

"OK, but I just read something very interesting, James!"

"No buts, Mrs. Steele."

I sat up. "But you'll like this! Listen! I was reading *A Death in Brittany...*"

"By Jean-Luc Bannalec?"

"Of course! You've read it?"

"No, but I read the review."

"Well, as I was saying--the plot revolved around a forged painting. (Rather timely!) And a curator from the Musee d'Orsay in Paris said that often forgers hid their names in the copies. Like a game! Like a joke!"

"Forget it, Mrs. Steele."

"But Commisaire Dupin found a name in the painting and solved the murder!"

"It's fiction! French fiction!"

"Oscar Wilde said life imitates art!"

"I do love Oscar Wilde," he said.

"I do love him, too."

Forty Five

I did not expect to meet him in the lobby. I was bedraggled. I didn't put on my bra, didn't put on my face, and didn't comb my hair. My Manhattan Portage bag was slung across my wrinkled tee, and I was clutching my uneaten lunch. I thought I'd fit right in with the public transportation crowd.

"Are you going back to work?" James asked looking a bit concerned as we walked to the exit.

"No, it's almost three. I called in sick. I'm…feeling…I want to keep feeling what I'm feeling."

He held my hand. We looked out the doors. Rain was pouring down.

"Where are you parked?"

"I took the bus."

"I'll drive you home. I'm in the parking structure."

We ran to the entrance next to Johnson Center. We rode the elevator.

"I'm on the roof," James said going up. We stood silently side by side.

The doors opened. Horizontal sheets of rain came down. "Run!" he yelled. He pointed to a black Jeep Commander.

"I thought you had a Passat?" I hollered as we ran.

"The Police Department leased this one! More muscle!"

"Hahaha!"

***

James bleeped the passenger door open. The front seat was piled with books, a laptop, files, and a briefcase. I screamed. "Get in back!" James shouted over the thunder. I got in the back seat. I was soaked. James got in the driver's seat. He started the car. I was laughing. He turned around.

"My lunch!" I said. I held up the soggy sack. James stared at me. I stopped laughing. His eyes narrowed. His long lashes were spiked from the rain. His eyes got even greener. I must look like a drowned rat, I thought. He turned off the ignition, bolted out the door and got in the back seat.

"Hungry?" I asked.

"Yes."

There was something about his look that made me put the bag between my teeth and crawl over to him. James reached for my lunch, dropped it on the floor and pulled me close. I leaned into his arms. He kissed me. I could not get enough He drove me crazy. I smelled chlorine on his skin and hair. We were both so cool and wet. Our breath was so hot. His hand moved slowly up my leg and under my dripping skirt. I pressed even closer to him. He began to gently move his lips over the tee shirt plastered to my breasts.

Rain pounded down on the car. My head fell back against the steamy window. I grabbed his shirt.

"Don't stop," I whispered.

"What?" he asked.

"That."

"This...or that?"

"Oh James..."

Forty Six

"I really need…," James said. I sat back against the door, bent my knees and tucked my feet under him. I threw my arms over my head. I breathed. I looked at him. I felt like I was in a dream. My gums were numb. How could his wife sleep her life away when she could have had this 24/7? I'll never understand marriage. Especially my own.

"Yes?" I finally sighed.

"I really need to…" He slowly moved his fingertips up and down my bare calves.

"Yes?"

"talk…"

"Yes?" I drew my feet out from under him and started to crawl.

"…about accounting."

I froze on hands and knees. "Great!" I said brightly. "But first excuse me. I was just going to get my lunch." I reached over his lap to get my lunch on the floor.

"You're excused," James said with a little smile.

I crawled back to my door. James pulled my feet under him again. I split the turkey sandwich between us that kept dry in a zip lock baggie. The rain had slowed down to a steady drizzle, we cracked the windows, and fresh air blew in.

We stared at each other while we ate.

"Well, go on," I finally said.

"A large amount of money was deposited in Roland's name in a Cayman Islands bank. Olive is also on the account," James said.

"Like I'm so surprised!" I snarked and offered him some Doritos.

"Money was withdrawn on a regular basis over the last year."

"Probably financing Olive's little gallery venture and house renovations."

"I have to find out where he got the millions he deposited there in the first place."

I popped open the Diet Coke. "Has to be art," I said.

"Forgeries?"

"Big business, James. And I bet you anything that it has something to do with Georgia O'Keeffe's work. And Charles knew it. Or was in on it with Roland. He had copies of proof of ownership in his locker! Who owns the authentic O'Keeffe paintings now?"

"Maybe Roland sold his own art and did not want to pay taxes."

"Leroy told me Roland was a terrible artist…"

"And you believe him?"

"I do! And if he did sell his work, he could never get that price for them! And how was the money deposited anyway?"

"It was done electronically from the Walters' home computer--transferred from money sent through Switzerland."

"We have to look closely at the Georgia O'Keeffe works in the Art Museum! To see if they're copies! The museum staff is at a conference all week and…"

"Stay away from those. Lt. Keyes and I will make arrangements…"

"As you wish, COMMANDER Hutchinson."

James suddenly lunged toward me and grabbed my shoulders.

"Don't play around, Mrs. Steele. I mean it."

I wiped the smirk off my face. I caught my breath. I did not breathe until he turned around, yanked open the door, slammed it and got in the driver's seat. That was himself putting his foot down. To say the least.

Forty Seven

I walked into a dark house. Faint music was coming out behind the boys' closed doors. Suki was happy to see me. Something! I let her outside. I turned on some lights, got a towel out of the bathroom, and went in my bedroom. I took off my damp clothes. I looked at myself in the mirror. I thought of James and flushed bright red all over. I had to snap out of it! But I didn't want to. I pulled on some yoga pants and a tissue tee. Now what...dinner.

I stood in front of the kitchen sink and stared out the window. Suki looked back at me. I let her in. Where was John? The house felt so different when he was gone. Like it opened up and sighed. Like it became so light and floated a bit off the ground.

"So where have you been?" Max asked.

I turned around. "Swimming. Then got caught in the rain. Had to wait. How are you, honey?" I kissed his head.

"Kale for lunch again?"

"Oh Max!"

"Dad had an emergency audit in Santa Fe. He'll be gone overnight."

"Oh! An emergency audit? That's a new one for the books!"

"Mom! Remember this is New Mexico State Government! Clever plans and nasty tricks!"

"Say no more. I understand now…" I laughed.

"And Peter called. He's got a bad virus or something."

"Oh God…I'll call him.

Douglas came in. "Thanks for your car, Mom."

"You're welcome." I hugged him.

"Dad took my car in to get fixed before he left. Can you please take me to Cataline's tomorrow morning before school?"

"Of course…Now what shall we eat?"

"Breakfast for dinner!" They said in unison.

***

After my bath I crawled into bed with my dog. I was concerned about Peter. He sounded so weak on the phone. He'd been to the Student Health Center. They told him to rest and drink plenty of fluids. He was still running a fever. I wished he were closer! Austin was so far away. His girlfriend was making him soup, he said. Peter told me not to worry. But I knew he had always been a stoic child and never complained. (He must have gotten a recessive gene. No one sniveled like John and me.) I'll call Peter again tomorrow. I had to take care of my family! Guilt washed over me. What was I doing with my life?

And what was with my Inspector's strong warning? Especially after being so...so very...affectionate. I felt his explosive energy like a lightning bolt. I knew he only wanted to keep me out of harm's way, but his outburst gave me a jolt--not that I was afraid that he would hurt me. I did wonder if this intensity, when unleashed, had the power to burn everyone and everything in its wake. Maybe that was why his wife slept so much. He exhausted her. Maybe that's what I felt in his touch. In his kiss. So different from John's. The power held in check under the surface.

He electrified me.

I did not want to think anymore, so time for *A Cinnamon Summer:*

"Brad is my husband!" Lily screamed. She pulled her curls! The dogs rushed to her whining with concern. She buried her head in Tulip's salty, wet fur.

"Your husband?" Chance exclaimed.

"I left him! We're separated! The divorce is not final! How did he find me?"

"Don't think about that now. We've got bigger fish to fry."

"And I need to know if my Aunt is all right! Oh Chance!!!"

"There's a phone at the Fire Department. Our cell phones are dead! Once we get to a safe place, I will go there and call Flo. This Brad is a maniac. You can't go back to Greenport!"

"Oh where can we hide?"

"*I have an idea. Let me see if I still have it.*" *Chance pulled a huge key ring out of his cut-off jeans pocket. He slowly turned each key over. This took a while. He had a large set of keys after all.*

(I bet he had quite a set.)

"*Yes! Here it is! Get to the car!*"

They stumbled and slid up the rocky hill. Lily could barely walk. Her feet hurt. She felt so weak.

"*He doesn't love me! Why is he looking for me?*"

"*Who knows? Get in the car!*"

They turned right on the small main road. They wound around beautiful trees. The quiet, perfectly groomed homes and grounds were left behind. Soon they came upon little gray cottages surrounded by narrow white sidewalks. Old-fashioned metal lawn chairs sat on each front porch.

"*Where are we, Chance?*"

"*Artist studios.*"

"*What?*"

"*For the William Steeple Davis Trust Artist-in-Residence program.*"

"*Who?*"

"*Some dead guy who left a lot of money. Artists apply to come here for a year to live and do their art rent-free. Long story! But hardly anyone ever applies. This place is empty most of the time. I did some plumbing here a week ago. I still have a key to number 7. Come on!*"

Chance parked on the side of cottage number seven hidden from the street. The dogs bounded out. Chance took Lily's hand and helped her out of the car. She was shaking with grief, fear and confusion. She was at the mercy of a long haired ex-con and running away from an abusive, violent husband. Where could she ever feel safe in this world? Lily decided that she had to trust Chance! What choice did she have? What a pickle!

Some pickle, Lily! We all have our crosses to bear! But I was truly grateful that John wasn't abusive or violent. Just an asshole.

I should have read more, but I needed to sleep. Worries about Peter made me toss and turn for a while--not to mention my new best friend: guilt. But hadn't I read somewhere that guilt was a useless emotion? I fell asleep.

Forty Eight

I sat at the Art Museum front desk and stared at all the students walking through the Fine Arts foyer. They all looked happy with their art portfolios and musical instruments. Did I see a tiny girl in black dart by? With inky black, shellacked hair? I wondered if she had sharp teeth. My imagination was running wild. Most Fine Arts students wore black. I was paranoid.

And I was so concerned about Peter. I had called him before I took Douglas to get his car. I told him to go back to the doctor since his fever had lasted over three days. He promised me that he would have his girlfriend take him. What could I do from here? I felt so powerless.

And alone in this museum. All the administrators were at a conference. Probably Linda was out somewhere refilling her gallon-sized soda container. My student helper Mike came in. Since we only had a few visitors,

I left him in charge and decided to take a little walk... around the museum. So my Inspector needed to "make arrangements" before looking at the Georgia O'Keeffes? With Ms. Keyes? Hell with that! I walked through the main gallery and out its back doors. I took a few steps across the short hallway and opened the doors to shipping and receiving with my master key. Now what? To the right was a huge freight elevator. I pushed the only button: downward arrow. The door opened. I stepped inside. Down I went and clunked to a stop. With only the light from the elevator I searched the walls on each side for an electric switch for the storage area. I finally found it. I was surrounded on both sides by floor to ceiling wrought iron fencing. Behind the fence I could see framed picture after picture stacked upright in separate cubbyholes of various lengths and widths. How does one get inside this cage to the art? I followed the concrete walkway looking for a gate, or something! I felt like I was in a dungeon. I had to go back, I thought. I started to panic. It was so cold down here with eerie dim lighting. But...I kept walking. I got goose bumps. Finally I saw a gate right in front of me. An entrance to both sides of storage. And a black box. With numbers. And a little blinking red light. Crap! I ran back to the elevator.

I collapsed in a chair beside Mike.

"What happened, Boss?" he asked.

"Oh I just went to Satellite for coffee."

"Looks like you've seen a ghost. I'd stay away from caffeine for a while."

Forty Nine

I could barely digest my sack lunch. I sat on the grassy slope outside the Fine Arts Center. I saw Linda walk by on her way to the Student Union Building. She did nod to me. Friendly, as usual. So the main office was empty now. I might just go see what I could see. I threw my trash away and walked quickly into the building and up to the office.

I was used to looking at four closed doors. Nothing new there. And I did have a master key. Was there a security code sheet somewhere? Everyone should have one! Even Linda! Or maybe not her. Linda came in as I was standing there thinking clever thoughts.

"What do you want?" she asked.

"Oh! I forgot my yogurt in the fridge!"

"Harrumph." She shuffled past me with her bag of McDonald's and sat down in her fortress.

I opened and closed the refrigerator door noisily and

left. I'd go downstairs to Ken's lair. He had to have a code! He was the Curator of Exhibitions!

Ken's large, airy, clean area was filled with long wooden tables, rulers, markers, wooden frames of every dimension, saws, and tools. It was a garage paradise. Colorful posters of musical groups hung on the walls. There was not a speck of dust on the floors or on any surface. I stood over his long work bench. He had two computers, a stereo system, stacks of CDs, tablets, pencils, and diagrams of the dimensions of each of the Art Museum Gallery walls. I started opening drawers. Clean, orderly, office supplies...but there was a CD of *Cajun Fire* by the Foulards lying under some post-it notes. Out of place? Ken! You're slipping, I thought nastily! I picked it up idly and opened the plastic case. The disc was not quite clicked into the circular holder. I lifted it up. There taped on the back was a sequence of numbers on a small piece of paper. Aha! I copied them into the Notes on my phone.

Now! I would try again! But first I had to check in with the museum front desk. Cathy and Alana were chatting it up--quietly. No one was in the museum. Slow day, thank goodness, for my purposes! I told them that I had to run some purchase orders for merchandise I had ordered over to accounting. I took the forms out of a drawer, opened another drawer and got a magnifying class. The students looked at me oddly. "My eyes are going bad! Getting old!" I said. I went out the front doors, walked around the entire building to the back loading dock, opened the door to the narrow hallway, and let myself into shipping and receiving.

Fifty

Down in the storage I punched the numbers into the security box with shaking hands. The red light turned green. The gate opened. Now what? So much art. So little time. By any chance could the works be alphabetized by artist? One could only hope. I started on the right side of storage. John Marin... Agnes Martin...I moved on. Then Nordfeldt...I was excited...and there she was! Georgia O'Keeffe's *Grey Hill Forms* and *White Flowers*. I must not have been breathing because I was faint-headed. I stood still for a moment and took deep breaths. My hands gripped the sides of the wrought iron bars of the cage. Then I carefully lifted out *Grey Hills Forms*. The light was so dim! I gently put it on the floor, sat down and took the magnifying glass out of my bag. I looked until my eyes started to water. The spring vegetation at the bottom of the eroding land forms had a few swirling dark brown branches in their light green foliage. I turned it upside down--a trick I learned in Drawing 101 to check perspective. In five of the shrubs I thought I saw "Chuck" spelled out: a delicate, curling branch forming a letter in each shrub. Were my eyes playing tricks on me? Wishful thinking? Nothing definite, but the forger could not be so blatant! I put *Grey Hill Forms* back. I took out *White Flowers*. Too much white. I could not see any letters in the leaves. I felt like I was going crazy looking for something that I had heard about in a French mystery. I was cold and tired. I put *White Flowers* back. So much for my grand ideas. I wanted to cry, but I heard a mechanical grinding sound. The freight elevator? I froze. My ears were ringing from nerves. I was scared. I quickly left the secured art area and walked to the elevator. The door was open. (Wasn't it closed before?) It was empty. I breathed a sigh of relief. I entered the elevator, pressed the up arrow, and went up and out.

***

My student helpers left at 3:00. I straightened up the shelves of merchandise and ran the credit card machine. I took the crumpled purchase orders that I said I was bringing to Accounting out of my bag and stuffed them back in a file. All the while I was thinking about whether I should tell my Inspector what I thought I saw in the painting. Should I call him? Oh this was such flimsy, wishful thinking evidence. Or was it? And he did not want me near the O'Keeffes. He made that clear. Let him and Ms. Lieutenant handle it.

But I called him anyway. No answer. I left a message: "The French may be right."

I logged onto the computer to see what was sold today. I was always surprised to see what was popular with the public. Like I thought the bleeding sacred heart tees were so "with it", but they were collecting dust. I got up to lock the museum doors at 4:00. Clarence sashayed around the corner. He pointed to me, then put his hands together in prayer, and mouthed 'please'. I unlocked the door.

"Get to work, Caro," he said.

"I am working! What are you doing wandering around?"

"Just taking a break..." He walked over to the bowl of rings on the counter. He tried a few on--holding his hand way out in front of him.

"Shopping?"

Clarence slowly took each ring off. "No. Actually I think you should know that Roland came in the Theatre Office and asked me questions about the police and you."

"What did you say?"

"I said that I did not know what was going on. Nobody tells me anything."

"And...?"

"He sat down by my desk and got all cozy. He still felt horrible about Charles's death. Blah...blah...so sad was Roland....He thought Inspector Hutchinson was having an affair with you and not concentrating on solving the murder--Caro, you little minx--He wants to file a complaint with the city police department. He wants him off the case."

"That asshole! And we are not having an affair!" Technically, I rationalized.

"You think I care? But don't say I didn't warn you, girlfriend."

"Thank you, Clarence."

"Loving these sacred heart tees!" He lifted one up in front of his chest. "Thank God you have a size small! I'll take it!"

Fifty One

I walked up Central Avenue to my car parked on the side of Walgreen's. The 5:00 traffic was awful. Central Avenue was becoming like Coors Boulevard. And all the bikers riding on the sidewalk! A hazard. I decided to go down an alley and walk up Silver. I loved alleys. I looked over fences. I ran my hands over bushes. I smelled flowers spilling over walls. I said a prayer for Peter. I tried to think of something to throw together for dinner. I heard rapid footsteps behind me. I turned. I saw a black blur. I felt a deep stab in my side. I fell-- My bag was yanked off me. I screamed. And screamed. A bicyclist rode down the alley. He was steering with one hand and talking on his cell phone with the other. He got off his bike, knelt down, took off his shirt and pressed it against my bleeding side. I was sobbing. I did not want to die. The pain! "Help is on the way," the good Samaritan kept saying.

"My little missy!" I saw Leroy fall to his knees next to me. He was weeping and moaning. "What did they do to you?"

I heard sirens. I saw a police car. Then a fire truck and an ambulance. Women and men rushed out of them. One applied pressure to my wound. I looked away from all the blood. Leroy kept wailing. The biker tried to comfort him. And lead him away from me. I started shaking. "She's going into shock," I heard. I was put on a stretcher and lifted into the ambulance. Then I was transferred to another surface where my legs were raised above my head. I surrendered. I had no control over my body or pain. I was so scared. I felt this way giving birth.

A man and a woman worked together quickly: one pressed gauze hard against my bleeding side while the other checked my vital signs, examined my entire body for other injuries, and placed oxygen tubes in my nose. They covered me with a blanket. The engine started. The back door closed. The ambulance started moving. The ambulance stopped. The back door opened. My Inspector charged in. I burst into tears. Again.

"Hey! Get out!" A man shouted.

I saw James flash his badge. "I need to be with her! She's a key witness in a murder investigation!"

"You can't question her now!"

"I won't!" James bent down...his face close to mine. Those eyes. "Don't leave me, Mrs. Steele."

"Never," I whispered.

Fifty Two

I opened my eyes.   Max and Douglas were sitting on each side of the bed.   They jumped up.

"Mom!"   They both said.   I saw John get up from a chair in the corner of the room.   He stood at the foot of the bed.

"Caro," John said.   "My God! How did this happen?"

"I was walking to my car…"   I whispered.

"I am going to pay for a parking place at the university if you insist on working there!   Walking through the ghetto?   What were you thinking?"

"Dad!   She just got out of surgery!"   Max exclaimed.

"Your mother was stabbed and robbed!   I cancelled all your credit cards, Caro."

I turned to Douglas.   "Am I all right?"

"Yes," he said.   "None of your organs were touched. The doctor will tell you everything.   You will be fine. Don't worry."

I started to cry. Max ran out of the room. "I'll tell the nurse that you're awake."

John walked up to the side of the bed. "There is a policeman sitting by your door. Why?" I stared at him.

"Dad! Enough!" Douglas said.

"I care! I want to know what is going on! I want to get to the bottom of this!"

I closed my eyes. I could not even look at John. I wished he'd shut up.

"Dad's just worried about you, Mom," Douglas said.

"I want a doctor in here, and I want him now!" John stormed out.

"The doctor is a woman," Douglas called after him.

I laughed, but it hurt. I sighed. I held Douglas's hand. "Here she is," he said. John and Max came with her.

Dr. Shannon looked like she was in middle school. "You are a very lucky woman, Mrs. Steele," she said. "The knife never punctured the serous membrane that protects your abdominal organs. The knife went through your oblique and transverse abdominal muscles. You have soft tissue damage. That's all."

"Thank God for my muffin top," I said.

"Well, the knife went a lot deeper than your muffin top, but with time you'll feel normal again." She smiled. "No Pilates!"

"Dang. My favorite pastime."

"You can go home tomorrow. I'll prescribe something for pain and a dose of antibiotics. I'll set up an appointment to see you in a week. Rest. Oh...I had to fill out a police report. We have to on all knife wounds."

"Thank you, Dr. Shannon," I said.

"Why is that policeman outside her door?" John asked her.

Dr. Shannon looked at him. "Mrs. Steele is a key witness in a murder investigation. Someone tried to kill her." She left. John turned to me.

"What have you done, Caro?"

"She discovered a very important clue, Mr. Steele." My Inspector walked in.

Fifty Three

My eyes filled with tears. James took a step towards me. John stepped in front of him.

"So we meet again. At another hospital when another member of my family was almost killed. So you're involved with this, too? I should have guessed!" John said.

"Mr. Steele," James said. "I am so sorry this happened. I am investigating a murder at the art museum where Mrs. Steele works. She has been very helpful..."

"I bet she has! She hasn't been herself at home! This is my family and..."

My sister flew into the room. "Oh Caro! What happened?" Sally ran to me. "Oh my God! I was in a meeting, then swam a mile, then out for drinks. Left my phone in the car under my coat! I didn't see Max's texts! Are you all right?"

"I will be fine. No major organs damaged."

"Oh Caro! This is terrible! How could this happen?" Sally turned to hug Douglas, Max, and John. She stopped in front of James. "And you are?"

"James Hutchinson."

"Oh, I've heard a lot about you! Well! Yes…Hmm… OK…" Sally kept looking at him. "I'm Sally. So what are you going to do about this? Do you have any suspects? How did you let this happen to my sister?"

"So you knew they were working together?" John asked.

"Caro told me a little something about him…" Sally turned back to James. "So you're from New Orleans? I was there after Katrina for a conference. So sad! But I have to say that I…"

"Excuse me!" I said. "I've been stabbed! Can we have a travelogue later? Please?"

My sister kissed me on the forehead. "I love you!" She turned around. "Come on, guys. I'll take you out to Slate Street for dinner." She shook James's hand. "So very nice to meet you." She glanced back at me with raised eyebrows. Max and Douglas kissed me good-bye. They shook hands with James.

"I'm staying here with my wife." John squeezed my hand.

"Ouch!" I said.

"Dad! Let mom rest. We'll come back in a while," Max said.

Everyone left. Except James.

He moved a chair close to me and sat. He took my hand, placed it on his cheek, then pressed his lips to my wrist. Tears started running down my face. He was so cool. "What am I going to do with you, Mrs. Steele?" he whispered.

"Anything you want," I said. He looked at my crumpled, bandaged body attached to wires and flashing machines with a little grin. "But not yet."

"Certainly not!" A nurse bustled in. "I'm going to check Mrs. Steele's vital signs. Then you have five more minutes. She needs her rest."

James held my hand while she did her thing. "Your temperature is up. This can be normal after your procedure. We'll keep an eye on it. Five more minutes, Inspector." She left.

I had to talk fast. "I turned *Grey Hills Forms* upside down, and I'm almost certain that I saw 'chuck' written in the branches of the foliage. Then I heard the freight elevator. Its door was open when I went back up to the front desk! I thought I'd closed it. I left you a message. I walked down an alley to my car. A black blur ran up behind me. Short. Just black!"

James stood up but still held my hand. "We got permission to remove the Georgia O'Keeffe paintings from the museum. Peter Eller Art Appraisers will look at them. Don't worry. Everything is going to be all right. Rest. I will be back tomorrow." He bent to kiss my forehead. "Good work, Mrs. Steele, but I do wish you would have listened to me," he said with his face close to mine. "And you are running a fever." I reached up and put my arms around his neck. I started to cry again. He gently lifted me up a little and hugged me. A machine started beeping. The nurse came in.

"Say good-bye, Inspector," She said as she untangled some wires and re-connected others.

Fifty Four

I had a painful, restless night. Off and on I slept but had horrible dreams. John came in early. I was looking sullenly at my breakfast tray of cream of wheat, orange juice and yogurt. He stood next to me with tears running down his face.

"We came back after dinner, but you were asleep. The nurse said no more visitors for the night. I am so sorry. I am so sorry. This is not your fault. I didn't mean to blame you. I love you, Caro. I can't live without you. I can't imagine life without you. When I thought you might die, I thought I would kill myself. Yes! I could not go on without you. Investigate, walk alleys, work at UNM! Just come home to me every night! I need you!"

I looked at his sorrowful face. He was suffering more than I was. It was all about him. I had to get his mind off himself.

"Have you heard from Peter?"

"Oh yes. He's got mono."

"Oh my God! Poor thing!" I cried. Again.

"I'm flying him home with a wheelchair assist."

"What?"

"Peter needs to be home for rest and care."

"Who will take care of him?"

"I am taking off. I will care for both of you. Douglas is moving into Max's room. They've already rolled out the lower trundle bed. I stored the drums in the garage. Peter will sleep in Douglas's room. My family will all be under one roof under my care."

I couldn't think of anything more horrible. I started having the chills. My teeth chattered. I was looking forward to Hell on Earth. John had never done grocery shopping. He's only cooked that one Chinese dinner in his life. After I had babies, and my mother was dead, John took off work but only polished bathroom fixtures. I'll have to rely on Max and Douglas. And my sister. Thank God. I calmed down a bit.

John turned to leave. "The boys will be here after school unless you're dismissed before that. Text me."

"When is Peter coming?"

"Tonight."

"This too much!" I cried.

"I can handle it! I'll pick you up today and bring you home! My wife!" John gave me a kiss and left.

"Please Jesus," I prayed. "Do something!" I started burning up. A machine buzzed. A nurse came in. She was a young red-head with a pony tail. She took my temperature.

"You have a high fever: 103 degrees. You have an infection. I'll call Dr. Shannon, but I think you will have to be on IV antibiotics for a while. No going home today."

I texted my family. And my Inspector. My prayer may have been answered in a strange way.

Fifty Five

I slept through *Hoda and Kathie Lee.* I awoke when the nurse came to insert the antibiotic IV in my arm. I was a mess. Max came in.

"Why aren't you in school?"

"Bomb scare."

"What?"

"I brought you something." He pulled Tina's novel out of his backpack and put it on the rolling tray. "Thought you might like a little light reading."

"Gee thanks. How did you get here?"

"Took the bus."

"That's always fun...Max, listen! You have to help out when Peter and I are home! Call Aunt Sally! Please..."

"Mom! Don't worry! I've already got menus planned! And have gotten a quart of happy, free-range chicken noodle soup from Sprouts today and a fresh baguette for tonight. I have a bunch of happy, organic baby romaine for a salad. We'll be all right! There's always carry out! You have to get well!"

"Your father makes me nervous."

"Mom! He wants to help. I'll keep him busy with yard work and picking up dog poop. He'll do all the laundry! He likes the washing machine! He won't bother you or Peter. He needs to feel needed, Mom. Douglas and I will take care of everything."

"You have to go to school."

"I'll get compassionate leave."

I laughed. It hurt. Max kissed me good-bye. I reached for *A Cinnamon Summer*. Oh God. What now? Oh yeah…driving to Orient, hiding in an artists' retreat cottage… Lily was in a pickle.

"I am walking to the Fire Department!" Chance said. "Don't open this door for anyone!"

The cottage smelled stuffy. Lily opened the windows. There was a small living room, lumpy furniture, rag rugs, a rickety table and chairs in the kitchen, one bedroom with a double bed and stained white chest of drawers, and a tiny bath. Lily looked in the linen closet. Thank goodness there were clean sheets and towels. She chose a lilac set of sheets. But they smelled musty. Lily always hung her sheets outside to dry in Dallas. She loved the fresh air aroma. Lily thought about what to do about this conundrum as she made the bed. At last she remembered her purse sized Aqua de Gio perfume in her African bag.

(I wear that scent! Was Tina still basing Lily on me? But I would never put decals on my toes! Or wear feathered mules! Or bake!)

She sprayed the sheets lightly with perfume. She shook out an Amish quilt she found folded at the end of the bare mattress and laid it smoothly over the sheets. She fluffed the pillows. Ah! Ready for... Then she felt guilty! And wanton. Oh well...

Lily walked like a somnambulist toward the kitchen. Tulip was curled up on the only stuffed chair, and Bruno was stretched out on the faded sofa. Lily had to laugh a little.

She put her hands on her hips as she looked at the kitchen: Gas stove, small fridge, sink, cabinets. There was a note on the counter top dated last week:
'Thank you for a wonderful year! I finished my novel! A miracle! I am a new woman! Please find some food I left. Sincerely, Jacqueline Anais Boyer. P.S. Your plumber was so nice!"

(Chance probably roto-rooted her drain.)

"I'm sure he was!" Lily huffed. In order to distract herself from the wild feelings she had thinking of staying in this cottage alone with Chance, Lily explored the kitchen. Did the manager clean out the food? Lily opened cupboards: flour, sugar, powdered milk, salt and pepper, baking soda, baking powder, and cinnamon! In the refrigerator Lily found condiments, butter, eggs and bacon. The little freezer had a pack of hot dogs. When Bruno and Tulip heard her rustling around in the kitchen, they jumped off the furniture and stood hopefully on each side of her.

"Well!" Lily said. "No dog food! I'll boil the hot dogs."
She filled a saucepan with water and put it on the floor. The dogs lapped it up at the same time.

"You will have to wait a while!" she said as she put some of the frozen franks in a pan of water over a burner. She turned on the oven. She filled up a juice glass with water, removed the flower from behind her ear, and placed it in the glass. Lily put it in the middle of the small dining table. She smiled with delight at the burst of orange joy. Then she put a little of this and a little of that in a bowl and made small flat balls out of the mixture with her hands. Lily placed them on a cookie sheet, sprinkled sugar and cinnamon over the tops and put them in the oven. The aroma of cinnamon scones soon filled the cottage.

Chance came through the door. He held his wadded up sweatshirt in both arms. He put it on the table.

Lily rushed up to him. She gripped his wife-beater tee. "How is my aunt?" she cried.

He put his hands on her shoulders. "She is resting comfortably. She has a concussion, some broken ribs, and a sprained ankle. Flo is staying with her at the hospital. Geneva is conscious and joking around. She could give the police a description. At least I'm not a suspect anymore!"

"Have they found Brad?"

"The police are on it. There is an all points bulletin out for any car with Texas plates."

"Oh my God!" She started to cry.

"Don't worry! I brought you something. Look what I picked." He unfolded his sweatshirt that held blueberries and raspberries.

Lily clapped her hands. "Oh Chance! Thank you! But your sweatshirt is all stained!"

(Instant tie-dye!)

He is thoughtful, Lily thought!

(Like James. He was there for me. In all my confusion. For all my fears. I still remembered the peach he shared with me. How I wanted to lick the juice off his lips.)

"What do I smell?"

"Cinnamon scones. I'll scramble some eggs for dinner."

"Hmmm," Chance murmured. He gave her a smoldering look. "Here." He fed her a blueberry. Lily fed him one. Chance put a raspberry in her mouth. He kept his finger on her tongue. Lily sucked it gently. Her eyelids fluttered. She went somewhere else. Chance slowly drew his finger out of her mouth. Lily's eyes opened. "You need to be kissed, and you need to be kissed well," he growled. He swept her up off the ground into his arms. He kissed her passionately. Lily wrapped her arms around his neck. Chance lowered her a bit so the toes on her left foot grazed the floor. She bent her right leg. She felt like she was ascending on fluffy clouds of bliss...on her way to paradise. His lips were soft but firm. He tasted like berries. Lily kissed him back passionately. Their tongues touched softly. No jamming. No cramming. Just luscious. She could not get enough.

(I know that feeling.)

Lily finally tore herself away when Bruno and Tulip started whining for their hot dogs. They laughed watching their hopeful prancing.

I put down the heavy tome when my lunch came: small chicken breast, green beans, rice pilaf, a roll, apple sauce and hot tea. I morosely chewed. I wanted a hot dog! With relish and Grey Poupon mustard and onions on a poppy seed bun. And a La Cumbre Elevated IPA. Oh yeah. I rolled the tray to the side and got up to go to the bathroom: pushing my antibiotic drip with one hand and holding the back of my sexy hospital gown closed with the other. My wound hurt with every step. I will never take walking for granted ever again. I will be thankful for every painless step! And every painless laugh!

I napped a while. I woke up and started reading. Well, of course Lily and Chance ended up in the double bed after dinner:

She had never had sex like this before. She finally knew what all the fuss was about! She screamed and screamed as she came and came. The dogs got disturbed. Chance had to comfort them and close the door before easing into bed to ravage Lily once again. He put his hand over her mouth to muffle more screams. She put her tongue through his fingers. Oh yes. They had a time together. Then Lily flipped Chance over and got on top. She had never done this with Brad, but now she had the instinct of a woman on fire. Chance drove her crazy.

(I'm certifiable.)

The dogs scratched on the door.

(God! How many times could one have sex in one night? Once again I started to dislike my friend Tina intensely. She must be writing what she knows! Doesn't everyone? I read on with great envy.)

Lily soaked her throbbing verdant garden in a warm bath. She hummed All You Need is Love. She dreamily washed out her underpants in the warm sudsy water. She sang DaDa DaDaDa as she hung them over the shower rod to dry.

(I dreamily remembered picking up my underpants off the floor of the Jeep Commander.)

Chance hopped in the tub causing the water to rise and slosh on the floor. They fell upon each with soap. Afterwards Lily brushed his beautiful hair. She found a lime green Scrunchie and bobby pins in her make-up bag. Soon Chance had a man bun. He said he'd have to think about that! Chance rubbed her bruised delicate feet with a tube of lavender lotion she carried in her purse. Lily opened the windows for the cool night breeze to float over the bed. Then they spooned the night away with a dog curled up on either side of them. When the sun rose, they nudged the dogs off the bed. Chance moved his lips slowly down to her--

I can't read this anymore in my condition. I put *A Cinnamon Summer* back on the side table. I was so hot. I still had a fever. Must be that.

I could have done a lot more in the back seat.

Fifty Six

The ponytailed nurse interrupted my erotic thoughts. She changed the dressing on my wound. "The redness has gone down. We'll see how you are tomorrow." She took my temperature. "Down to 100 degrees. You're getting there, Mrs. Steele!" She left. I started thinking about Peter flying in tonight without me to greet him. Once again I felt like everything was too much to handle. I felt useless. And I hurt. I was no help to anyone. I started to cry. I was in the slough of despond.

I heard my Inspector talking to the policeman outside my door. I blew my nose and dried my eyes. James came in carrying a bunch of tea roses.

"The two Georgia O'Keeffe paintings in the museum are forgeries."

"Oh! James! I did something right!"

"Indeed you did."

I reached for the flowers. "Careful," he said. He held them for me while I buried my nose in soft petals.

"These are my favorite. Thank you. How did you know? And don't tell me you investigate!"

"I did investigate, Mrs. Steele. And Max told me."

"Oh him!"

James filled up my water pitcher in the bathroom. He arranged the roses inside it. He left and came back with another pitcher filled with water.

"We are trying to locate the original O'Keeffes. Our forensic accountant is tracing the Swiss account that paid the Walters millions. Roland has been brought in for questioning."

"Good! Was it 'Chuck' in the brambles that clued Peter Eller in?"

"No, actually, it was the type of paint. He had some chemical explanation. Georgia O'Keeffe used a certain type of pigment. These had a different composition."

"Sounds complicated. I liked the "Chuck" clue better."

"Mr. Eller did not mention it."

"He needs to read *A Death in Brittany*."

"He'd love that suggestion, I'm sure. How's your fever?"

"It's going down."

"Good." James held my hand in both of his and that made me get all weepy again. "What's wrong?"

"My son Peter is flying in from Austin tonight. He has mononucleosis. I am so worried about him."

"My daughter had that. The only treatment is rest, fluids, Advil, and time. He will be fine, I promise. Don't worry. You need to heal."

"Your daughter?"

"Yes, my daughter."
"What's her name?"
"Claire."

***

I wanted to talk more about this surprising piece of information, but the nurse came in to do something with my body. James kissed me on the forehead and left. "You're husband is very handsome," the nurse said.

"Yes, he is," I answered. Which was really true, I thought.

Fifty Seven

I started to pick up *A Cinnamon Summer* but let it flop back on my tray with a thud. Why should I be so surprised to hear that James had a family? I knew so little about him. But I have time. I will take the time. If he wants to talk, that is. I will wait and see. *Poco y poco*...little by little if we are meant to be.

But now I wanted to know why Charles was killed. And who did it? All evidence pointed to him copying the O'Keeffes. Roland sold the museum originals to an unknown party for millions. The money trail lead first to Roland and Olive and then to Charles's account. Charles could afford to build his cabin. But it burned down. I wondered if Olive had anything to do with that? Wouldn't surprise me. But I couldn't let my imagination run away with me. Oh why not? What else have I got to do?

I guess I had to eat my dinner: Yummy-do. Meat loaf, mashed potatoes, squash, fruit cup, sherbet, and hot tea. It was actually pretty good. I watched *Jeopardy* and felt like an idiot. My sister called. Peter was home and in bed. Sally said Max and Douglas bought happy chicken noodle soup from Sprouts. John served ice cream and cleaned up. She told me not to worry. She was going to stay at my house until Peter was asleep. She hoped to see me tomorrow. She loved me. She thought my Inspector was hot.

Yes, he was. I leaned over to smell the roses on the side table. It hurt. I fell back against the pillows. I was so thankful my sister was there with everyone. Sally was more than an aunt, more than a grandma, more than a mother to my boys. There should be a name in our culture for women like her.

But where was I? Thoughts forming in my head. I rolled my tray aside. I stared at the ceiling. OK… Charles was homeless. Out of money. No job. He could have still lived on his land in El Morro. In a tent? But he came back to roam around the University. To harass Roland? To blackmail Roland? And his charming wife? Charles needed more money! Wouldn't Leroy have told me if his friend Charles was blackmailing the Walters? Would he even know? When did Charles copy the O'Keeffes anyway? After he was fired? Roland threw him a bone? That was when he built his cabin. I'd better text James with my ideas. I'd love to know what Roland is saying to the police right now. Asshole.

I got out of bed to brush my teeth. I went into the

bathroom rolling my antibiotic bag and IV drip along. My wound hurt. My head was itching. I shuffled out of the bathroom only to see Olive sitting next to my bed.

Fifty Eight

"Olive?" I gasped.

"Well, aren't you a picture."

The room reeked of her Joy perfume. My eyes started to water. She wore a lime green tracksuit and black suede and silver high-top tennis shoes. Two red chopsticks stuck out of her platinum French Roll. I glanced out my open door and saw the guard sitting in a chair. Good. "What do you want, Olive?"

She got up and squeezed my upper arms with her long, Vamp polished fingers. "I am so sorry that you got mugged! This city!" I couldn't move. "Now you get settled in bed so we can have a little chat." She gave me a push. "I brought you a present!" Olive reached inside of her huge purse and brought out a bottle of Tanqueray gin. "Miss Manners wrote that instead of flowers one should bring a bottle of gin to someone in the hospital."

"Did she now," I said.

"Let's have a little toast to your health." She pulled two plastic glasses out of her cavernous bag.

"I'm on pain meds."

"Now, now. A little snort won't hurt…"

"I…" Olive splashed some gin in the glasses and handed me one.

"Let's toast to…oh…not your health right now, dear Caro, but let's toast your delightful Inspector." She clinked my glass and took a swig. I stared at her. "Well, drink up! I know about you two. Don't give me that deer caught in the headlights look."

"You don't know anything, Olive."

Olive smirked. She started pacing around the room. "Let me tell you a little bedtime story. I was married to a very talented artist. I took menial jobs to support us while he painted until he got an academic position. He left me for another woman after many years of marriage. I know…cue the violins." She poured herself another glass of gin. She walked to the window and looked out. "Roland and I had something in common: We were both betrayed by Charles. Anne left him for Charles. Charles left me for Anne. We were a match made in heaven."

Match made in a hotter place, I thought.

Olive knocked back the rest of her gin and sat on my bed.

"You can't sit on my bed," I said.

"I don't give a fuck. I soon found out that Roland had huge gambling debts. I'm not talking about poker night with buddies, but internet gaming, casinos, gambling in Las Vegas when I thought he was somewhere on museum business. But nobody's perfect. Right, Caro? But it was tough going for a long time. And poor Charles lost his job at the university. Very hard on him financially. It's amazing to think now how both the men in my life needed money at the same time. I had to be the creative one--think outside the box--imagine me advising two artists. But this plan used both their talents and connections. And my idea was a wild success for all of us...for a long time...until..." Olive looked at me while she crushed the plastic glass in her fist and threw it against the wall.

"You should write a memoir," I said.

Olive pulled a chopstick out of her French roll. She pressed an end with her fingertip. "What did you tell Inspector Hutchinson about Roland?"

"Nothing."

"The police picked him up this afternoon for questioning."

"Sad."

"I don't like liars, Caro." She emphasized each word by jabbing the chopstick in front of my face.

"I don't like murderers, Olive." I was about to call the guard.

She jammed the chopstick into the pitcher of tea roses and leaned over me. I looked at her ropy neck. Smelled her gin breath. "You really piss me off," she whispered.

A nurse came in. Olive started fluffing my pillows. "Take care, darling one," she purred and left.

Fifty Nine

I could only hope the pain meds helped me sleep. My heart was pounding. I texted my Inspector: 'Olive was here! Freaked me out!' I finally drifted into blessed unconsciousness.

A loud crash followed by a siren woke me up. I saw nurses and the police guard run by my door. What the...? I was groggy. Was I dreaming? A new nurse came into my room.

"What's going on?" I asked.

"Fire alarm." She took the bag of antibiotic off the stand and detached it from the tube leading to my IV needle. She hung up a fuller bag. She had to stand on her tiptoes. What a tiny nurse I woozily thought.

"Is there a fire somewhere?"

"I doubt it. False alarm probably. Don't worry, Caro." She struggled trying to reattach the tube to the needle in my arm.

The other nurses called me Mrs. Steele. And why was she so clumsy. I reached over to turn on my light.

"Thanks, Caro!" The nurse smiled, showing sharp teeth.

I sat up, grabbed *A Cinnamon Summer*, and threw it at her head. She fell to the floor. "Bitch!" she screamed. I got out of bed, poured the pitcher of roses on her face, and kicked her stomach. That hurt! She started choking. I limped to the door and yelled for help. I saw my Inspector running down the hall toward me. The police guard followed behind dragging a struggling Olive. I was tackled from behind. Damn that hurt! I landed on my hands and knees and collapsed on my uninjured side. James rushed in, picked up the kicking hissing girl and threw her in a chair. He noticed the bag of antibiotics on the floor. "She put a new bag on the stand!" I gasped.

The girl jumped out at James with a knife. He knocked the knife out of her hand with one hand and squeezed her neck with the other. She slumped to the ground.

"Did you kill Holly? Animal!" Olive screamed. She pulled another chopstick out of her do and tried to stab the guard in the eye. He ducked. James twisted her wrist. I heard a crack. The chopstick fell to the floor. He kicked it out of the way. "You broke my wrist!" He cuffed her to a chair. "Get me a doctor!" Olive cried.

James carefully lifted me off the floor onto the bed. He staggered. I was a sturdy woman, so to speak. "Get someone for Mrs. Steele," he panted to the policeman.

"Wait…" He took the new bag of antibiotic fluid off the stand. "Have this tested."

"How dare you treat me this way! I want my lawyer!" Olive said. "I'll sue you for every dime you have, you Cajun fraud. I know why you left New Orleans! You…"

A nurse came in. She looked at everyone with wide eyes then stared at Holly on the floor. "She'll wake up in a while," James said.

The nurse carefully checked my wound. "The stitches haven't been broken." She took my vitals. "No fever but elevated blood pressure." She drew the curtain around my bed and changed my dressing. She pulled the curtain back, gave everyone a withering look and left.

A man in a lab coat walked in. "I have some news about your IV drip, Mrs. Steele."

Sixty

"The bag contained ethylene glycol also known as anti-freeze."

"Oh my God!" I screamed.

"It's not lethal in itself, but over time, it metastasizes, changes, in the body to cause widespread tissue injury to the kidneys, liver, brain, and blood vessels," the coated one intoned. "It's fatal over time," he added.

"Thank you," my Inspector said. The technician leaned against the wall watching the dramatic tableau. "You can go now." He left.

James turned to Olive: "So your little friend wanted to do Mrs. Steele in?"

The little friend sat up. She rubbed her throat. "What happened?" she croaked.

"You tried to poison Mrs. Steele and stab me. If your knife was the same one used on Mrs. Steele in the alley..."

"She made us do it!" Holly cried, pointing at Olive.

You were so right, Leroy, I thought!

"She's out of her mind!" Olive said.

"You paid Hyacinth and me to do your dirty work! I am not taking full blame!"

"She's crazy! Delusional!"

"I'm not going down for your sake! I saved all of your texts and recorded our meetings on my IPhone!"

Those girls weren't that stupid, I marveled.

My Inspector's phone rang. He stepped outside briefly and returned. "Roland has confessed to selling the museum's O'Keeffe paintings to a Chinese-American who lives in Plano, Texas."

Olive shrieked: "He caved. The weak bastard. All I've known are weak bastards!"

"We would have found out eventually. Congress can track American citizens' Swiss bank accounts now," James said.

"But you have nothing on me!"

"But I do!" Holly shouted hoarsely. "Olive hated Charlie! She paid Hyacinth and me to falsely accuse him of harassment! Then when he threatened to go to the University Administration about Roland selling museum art unless Roland paid him more money for copying the O'Keeffes, she decided to kill him. 'No one will care about a dead homeless man,'" she said.

Overflowing with the milk of human kindness, as usual, I thought.

"Shut up, you little bitch!" Olive cried. "As if anyone would believe you! I found you and your sister working

Central sipping Big Gulps. Both of you have rap sheets a mile long."

Holly pointed a shaking finger at Olive. "She lured Charlie down to the lower museum gallery one night. Told him Roland had hung some of his paintings. He was so happy."

Roland did not hesitate seizing the art Charles left in his office. I wondered if Roland could ever have enough--especially art created by others. I realized Roland was a cypher.

Holly's face turned purple with rage. "Hyacinth and I were waiting. We knocked Charles down. Olive pulled a hammer out of her purse and hit him again and again."

"Hell hath no fury like a woman scorned" immediately came to my mind.

"Then you put his body in the handicapped lift," James said.

"Yeah…we did. He was so light. A bag of bones."

"You can prove nothing," Olive said.

"But you left something behind, Olive," I whispered.

She whipped her head around and hissed: "What?"

James answered. "I have a copy of a receipt from Beauchamp's Jewelers." James pulled a piece of paper out of his pocket. "Replacing ½ carat ruby in ring for a Mrs. Roland Walters," he read.

"You're pathetic! What are you getting at?"

James reached in his pocket again. "Perhaps to replace this one, Olive?" He held up the ruby.

"Big deal, Inspector! Is that all you have? I'm trembling in my Jimmy Choos."

"You should be," I said. "We found that in the handicapped lift."

"Inconceivable! You think I would ever get on that nasty thing? You could have gotten that red glass out of a Cracker Jack Box!"

"I think not." James turned the ruby over in front of his eyes. "It's real. And it was cut to fit in your skull ring's eyes. The jeweler agreed since he had to cut the new ruby exactly like this one."

Olive screamed, "Someone took that ruby out of my jewelry box and planted it in the handicapped lift! That coward Roland!" Then she pointed at James. "No! You framed me! You'd do anything to solve a case, wouldn't you?"

James turned his back on her and faced Holly. "I am arresting you on two charges on the attempted murder of Mrs. Steele, assaulting a police officer..."

"No! I did not stab her!"

"Seriously?" I said. "Then who did? I want my Manhattan Portage Bag back!"

James took a deep breath. "Holly, I am arresting you now on one charge of attempted murder of Caroline Steele, assaulting a police officer and one charge of accessory to the murder of Charles Lowry. You have the right to remain silent..."

"Fat chance!" Olive yelled.

"Cuff the girl," James said to the guard. "Put out an APB on her sister Hyacinth--what's your last name, Holly?"

"I refuse to answer on the grounds that it may incriminate..."

"It's Camry like the car," Olive snarled.

Once again James faced Olive and Holly. He read each of them their rights. Uninterrupted.

Sixty One

My head was spinning after everyone left. I hoped the meds started kicking in so I could sleep. I thought about James. The case was over. He would go back to New Orleans. Like last time. We had another moment together. And that was that.

A custodian came in to clean up the spilled water, crushed cup, chopsticks and scattered roses. I asked her for one and placed it next to my pillow. I drifted into unconsciousness thinking of James and was grateful.

***

I woke up early the next morning. I saw Douglas sitting in one chair reading *Hitch 22* and my Inspector sitting in another chair doing a crossword puzzle. I was surprised.

"Mom!" Douglas jumped up and hugged me. "Inspector Hutchinson told me everything that happened last night. I'm so glad you're OK!"

"Thank you, honey," I kissed him. "I am, too!"

"I'll help you check out. Dad dropped me off and went back to make Peter breakfast. I'll text him when you are ready to leave. I brought some clean clothes for you. Can I get you a breakfast burrito? Inspector?"

"Yes, please," we said. James gave him some money. Douglas thanked him and went down to the cafeteria.

I sat up. My Inspector pulled a cup of Satellite Coffee out of a bag and brought it to me.

"Thank you!" I said. We looked at each other. Then we laughed. I had not bathed and my hair was a greasy mess. I'd worn the same hideous hospital gown for three days. His hair was sticking out, his clothes were wrinkled, and he had a (quite sexy) stubble. I realized that he had worn the same clothes three days in a row. Not like him at all. "So I see you're sporting a Leroy vibe."

"Thank you very much, Mrs. Steele. I have been sleeping in the doctor's lounge ever since you were admitted."

"So that's why you got to my room so fast! Oh James!"

"After I got your text about Olive, I was on my way to you when I saw her in the gift shop holding a doll. Then the fire alarm went off, Olive saw me, and ran out of the shop. But I caught her."

"Of course you did. My Inspector..." I sighed dramatically, batted my eyelashes and got all dreamy eyed--as much as I could looking like a fright night.

James gave me a puffy, bloodshot smoldering gaze. We were a match made in heaven. Or somewhere.

Sixty Two

Douglas texted John when I was discharged. He and James followed the nurse pushing me in a wheelchair down to the hospital front door.

Suddenly James said: "I have to ask Mrs. Steele a few more questions about a murder case. Is there somewhere quiet we can go for a few minutes?" The nurse pointed to a conference room down the hall. James steered me into the room and shut the door. I stepped out of the wheelchair and fell into his arms. I hugged him so tightly. He held me so gently.

"I have to talk to you," he said in my ear.

"About accounting?" My question was muffled in his neck.

James pulled back so our faces were almost touching. He smiled. "No."

"Thank goodness."

"I have to go back to New Orleans."

"I know."

"And you have to take care of yourself and your family."

"James, I want…"

"*I* want you…" He kissed me. "healed, Mrs. Steele."

We heard a knock on the door and "Your husband is here". He lowered me slowly into the wheelchair. I couldn't let go of him. Another knock. I let him go. James opened the door.

The nurse rolled me out into the sunlight where John and Douglas were waiting.

Sixty Three

Max was right. John did love that washing machine. He kept Peter's fever soaked sheets and all our clothes laundered. He scooped up dog poop from the back yard everyday, vacuumed, did dishes, emptied trash cans, sorted recycling items and played his harp at night after Peter and I went to bed. My sister brought soups. Max made beans and chili and *Pollo con Naranja y Limon*. John got carry out. Douglas did the grocery shopping after school and band practice. And the pharmaceuticals helped.

Peter and I spent the first week we were home in a daze re-watching all the seasons of *Twin Peaks* on Netflix and napping. He was so weak. His high school friends heard he was back in town. They'd call first to see when they could visit. I felt so relieved to hear him laugh with them. Peter started feeling stronger after about two weeks. Douglas drove us to the Ernie Pyle Library. We checked out lots of books to read. Peter was in e-mail contact with his professors at the University of Texas. They agreed to let him finish his incompletes during the upcoming summer session. Peter was anxious to get back to Austin and his girlfriend.

The Art Museum administrators sent a bouquet of tulips. The work studies wrote personal messages in a beautiful card. Pat and Linda (!) came to visit me. They brought a bag of Chick-fil-A for lunch. And big Cokes. And a piece of art from Leroy. He had drawn a sketch of me sitting at the museum front desk. "Come back soon, Little Missy" he wrote on the bottom. The museum was holding up. Since Roland resigned in disgrace, the Dean of Fine Arts closed the downtown satellite. Pat was back at the main museum part-time. The wonderful students filled in the rest of the open hours. I was on temporary leave for as long as I wanted.

My friend Tina called to see if I could meet and discuss *A Cinnamon Summer*. I told her what had happened to me. She was shocked. I said that I could meet in a week. I hauled the manuscript in bed with Suki that afternoon. I read: *Ok...The sun rose...Lily and Chance got out of bed... finally! He took the dogs for a run. Energetic guy...She was mixing a little bit of this and that in a bowl for breakfast...sprinkling cinnamon here and there...yes...yes...good little baker...Then...Oh no!*

The screen door crashed open. Brad stormed in. Lily screamed. He grabbed her hair. "Where are they?" he yelled.

"Where's what?" she cried.

"My computer files!"

"What are you talking about? Ouch! You're hurting me!" She whacked him on the nose with a wooden spoon. Brad shook his head but held on to her hair. Lily kneed his groin. He doubled over in pain. Lily ran out the door. Brad shuffled after her. In spite of his agony, he was in good shape from running all over Dallas with a tire chained around his waist. He caught up to her, pushed her to the ground, pulled a knife out of his belt and held it to her cheek.

"All the files in my computer are gone! Now tell me where they are, or you will need major plastic surgery."

"I don't want your stupid files. I just downloaded my recipes!"

"You downloaded all the folders! The computer is wiped clean, you stupid bitch! Where are your damn recipes?"

"On my zip drive. In Aunt Geneva's cottage!"

"Jesus Christ!" Brad snarled then screamed with pain when Bruno and Tulip flew through the trees and sank their teeth into his hard flesh. Brad tried to raise his knife to stab them when Chance came out of nowhere and karate chopped the knife out of Brad's hand. Lily heard a crack.

"You broke my wrist!" Brad screamed. He still tried to choke Lily with his other beefy hand. Chance squeezed Brad's thick throat. He collapsed unconscious.

(Like my Inspector! Whatta guy!)

Chance gently lifted Lily into his arms and carried her back to the cottage.

"I can walk, Chance," she said weakly.

"No way," he murmured in softly in her ear. "You're as light as a feather, my precious one."

(Oh! I thought of my Inspector staggering while carrying me a few feet to the hospital bed.)

He held her shaking body so tenderly. She cried hot tears into his hoodie. They heard a siren.

Chance and Lily sat holding each other tight in the Orient Fire Station with a Sgt. Montgomery from the Suffolk County Police. Lily still had a few twigs in her hair. Chance gently picked them out every so often. Her white dotted swiss shirt was torn. Her madras shorts were smeared with mud. She was missing one flip-flop. The dolphin decals had peeled off her toes. Her face was tear stained.

"Well, we got an APB from Dallas about this Brad character. A sorry piece of work. One of our patrols spotted his car with the Texas plate. We followed him to Orient. He lost us in the Artist Retreat labyrinth. But we finally found his parked car."

"How did he know we were here?" Lily asked as she still clung to Chance.

"Brad went to the only service station in Greenport. He said that he was searching for his runaway bride and her boxer! The guy told him that a guy had filled up a white Fiat 500 with a woman in the car and a boxer in the back seat who turned north out of town. The only place north of Greenport is Orient. And Plum Island. But no one can go there! He told us Brad drove a black Lexus."

"Bastard!" Lily cried.

"Yes, Ma'am, a nasty piece of work. He and his real estate partner have run a home equity scam across Dallas.

They stole elderly homeowners' identities, applied for home equity loans in the victims' names, even sold some homes out from under them, and split the money. A sad state of affairs. Not to mention what he did to Geneva! Well...I just got word from the Riverhead Jail that Brad regained consciousness..."

Harrumph, I thought as I slammed the manuscript shut. Art scams were much more dramatic!

Sixty Four

The next week my stitches came out. The wound healed up. I eventually had no pain and just a little tenderness. I felt very lucky. Peter and I started taking Suki for short walks. The fresh air and sunshine were good for us. I slept peacefully with John. He only scratched my back sometimes. He knew what I liked.

But I still had an itch.

Tina came over with cassoulet and homemade cinnamon rolls. She was beautiful in a Mexican embroidered maxi dress. I wore Gap plaid pajama bottoms and hoodie.

I hugged her. "Oh Tina! Thank you!" I pointed to the rolls. "And life imitating art!"

Tina laughed. "Dear Oscar Wilde!"

We had coffee and a plate of Oreo Thins in the den. John had started working again. Thank goodness.

Max and Douglas were in school. (I hoped!) Peter was napping. Quiet. We could talk.

"I'm so sorry," I said, "but I haven't finished your book…"

"Don't worry about it, Caro! You've been rather busy and distracted, to say the least! Spoiler alert: Lily and Chance live happily ever after with their two children in Greenport where she bakes every day for Flo, and Chance starts a landscaping company and is elected mayor."

"Fabulous! Happy for those two! Well, here are my notes." Tina stuffed them unread in her purse.

"Well? I suppose your Inspector Hutchinson was involved with all this museum business," she said.

"Yes. Oh Tina! I'm…he's….I never…" I choked up.

"Caroline Steele! Listen to you! Something happen?" Silence. "Between you?" Tina persisted.

"We made out. Or whatever it's called now. Or do modern lovers not pass go and just hook up?"

Tina rolled her eyes. "One misses so many erotic opportunities." She broke apart an Oreo and slowly licked the icing.

"I'll say." I stuffed an Oreo in my mouth.

"How was James?"

I swallowed. "Luscious."

"And you want more?" she asked.

"I want more."

"Then you should have it."

"And all the guilt of infidelity."

"You need to have fidelity to yourself, Caro."

Sixty Five

What I had in the next month was such relief that Peter
was well enough to return to Austin. I was also working
part-time again which was good to maintain balance
in my life--such as it was. The Art Museum hired a
young man to job share with me. Bradley used to work
at the Gift Shop at the Albuquerque Museum. He was
back at UNM to work on his degree. He had a great eye
for merchandise. Pat finally got a full-time position at
St. Martin's Hospitality House. The days went by. My
home was calm. Too calm. I was comfortably numb.
Then I got a surprise.

A thick, ivory engraved envelope came addressed to
me in the mail. It was an invitation from The Georgia
O'Keeffe Museum in Santa Fe to attend a celebration
in Abiquiu, New Mexico, honoring those who had
helped recover the original O'Keeffe paintings. The
invitation included dinner at the Abiquiu Inn, a night

in one of their casitas, and a tour of Georgia O'Keeffe's house. I mailed back my RSVP immediately. John said he wanted to go. He was worried about me driving up north. I told him that I needed time to myself after all the excitement of the last few months, and I could drive just fine. He said he understood. Thank God. Then Max wanted to go! I said no even though he pestered me for days: He needed to go because he was doing a research paper on Georgia O'Keeffe for English, he was studying fauna of the southwest for Biology, he was writing a paper on the Treaty of Guadalupe for History…then he finally said: "Have fun, Mom!" and gave me a hug. Oh! That boy will do me in yet!

On the day I left I dressed in slim jeans, a black tunic and boots. I took my mother's gray poncho for that ye olde Abiquiu look. I put a change of underwear in my purse. I backed out of the driveway and drove to the airport.

Sixty Six

I pulled into the parking structure. I re-read the text: Southwest flight 337 4:00. I rode the escalators up to the waiting area just outside of the security zone. I saw him walking down the long hallway. James came through the revolving doors and into my arms.

"How are you, Mrs. Steele?"

"I'm healed, Inspector Hutchinson."

We kissed passionately. When we finally broke apart people were staring.

**

The drive to northern New Mexico was lovely. The light was so beautiful. After turning northwest of Espanola and leaving behind all the low-riders, we had an empty highway and grand vistas: Colorful mesas, stately cottonwood trees, grazing horses and sheep. James thought it looked like the English countryside.

He asked about Peter. I asked about Claire. She was a junior at Colorado College. He asked about Max. He asked about Douglas's music. We talked about England and New Orleans.

Then we got down to business. James told me that while the Albuquerque Police searched the Walters' home, Lt. Keyes led a team that scoured the Art Museum for the murder weapon. They tested every hammer in Ken's garage. ("That must have been an all day job!" I interrupted.) One had minute traces of blood which matched Charlie's blood type. Holly and Hyacinth testified against Olive. Phone texts and recordings validated their statements. Holly ratted on her sister for stabbing me. Olive had told Hyacinth to make it look like a robbery. Olive later confessed to the murder of Charles Lowry.

Roland protested that he knew nothing about Charles's murder. Olive swore that she acted alone.

"Do you believe that?" I asked.

"Not really," James shrugged.

"Olive carried out the clever plans and nasty tricks in that marriage," I said. "She wanted to keep what she had. At any cost! I think Roland was happy to collect money, be a figurehead in the Art Museum, and play tennis. He couldn't be bothered. He is a lazy, weak man with a gambling addiction married to a shrewd, strong enabling woman."

"If Roland did know that Olive murdered Charles, he chose to ignore it so he could continue living a life of ease," James said.

"I guess we'll never know."

"Not yet, Mrs. Steele."

"I do know that Olive will not be thrilled wearing an orange prison jumpsuit!"

James laughed. "Definitely not her color!"

As we chattered away, all I wanted to do was pull off the highway onto a dirt road and do something with him. But I didn't.

Sixty Seven

We arrived at the small town of Abiquiu surrounded by red-rimmed cliffs. I parked in front of the Inn: a rambling adobe hacienda. Over to the right were the single casitas. We got out of the car and inhaled the cool air with the slight smell of pinon smoke. "This is magical," James said.

We walked in the lobby to shouts of "Here they are!" A waiter came over with glasses of champagne. The director of the Georgia O'Keeffe Museum rushed through the crowd to greet us. We were ushered into the dining room where we saw Peter Eller holding court around a table. Lt. Jane Keyes walked up to us with a nice looking older man. "Look who I brought!" she said.

The man gave me a hug. "Hello, Little Missy."

"Leroy!" I exclaimed.

"I got him an invitation," Jane said. "He told you so many important facts, Caro, which helped solve the murder and art forgeries."

"He did!" I gave him another hug. "You look great!" My eyes filled with tears.

"Got some teeth and dried out. St. Martin's helped me find a job teaching drawing at the Community College. Pat took care of me."

"I am so proud of you!"

"I'm proud of you, too, Caro," Leroy said.

"Thank you, Leroy." James shook his hand.

James steered me over to introduce Marc the young forensic accountant who chased Roland's money trail from Switzerland to the Caymans.

The University Art Museum Assistant Director and Registrar gave us queenly waves from their table. I briefly wondered why they were here. But whatever, I thought with a burst of benevolence. I was too happy.

Before dinner was served, a member of the Georgia O'Keeffe Foundation stood up to give a toast: "To Inspector James Hutchinson and Caroline Steele. Thanks to your hard work, persistence, curiosity, and bravery we have Georgia's paintings back where they belong."

"Here, here!" everyone shouted. James stood up and raised his glass. "Here's to French fiction!" Silence. I laughed.

"*A la votre*," Leroy yelled.

"*Sante*," James said.

Then everyone cheered even though confused.

Sixty Eight

I woke up. I was in a dream. A beautiful dream.

Slivers of moonlight shined through the blinds. Wood still flickered in the Kiva fireplace. I gently moved his hand from my breast. I got out of bed. I opened the shutters wide and unlocked the window. Fresh crisp air filled the room. The moon cast ghostly shadows off the sagebrush. An otherworldly glow bathed the craggy hill where Georgia O'Keeffe once lived.

I had an otherworldly glow.

James wrapped my mother's poncho around me.

"Can you see the moon?" I whispered.

"I can see, Caro."

THE END

CPSIA information can be obtained
at www.ICGtesting.com
Printed in the USA
FFHW021647190619
53090166-58740FF